D1398510

SPECTRUM

Geography

Grade 3

Published by Spectrum
an imprint of Carson-Dellosa Publishing LLC
Greensboro, NC

Spectrum
An imprint of Carson-Dellosa Publishing LLC
P.O. Box 35665
Greensboro, NC 27425 USA

Printed in Minster, OH U.S.A. • All rights reserved.   ISBN 0-7696-8123-9

4 5 6 7 8 9 10 11 GLO 14 13 12 11 10   14810019763

Table of Contents

Introduction to Geography

Types of Communities

Landforms and Water Forms

Early Communities

Connections to the Land

From Coast to Coast

Models of Earth

Geography is the study of Earth in all its variety. When you study geography, you learn about Earth's land, water, plants, animals, and people. One way to learn about Earth is to understand what it looks like.

A **globe** is a model of Earth that is round like a ball. It shows what Earth looks like. Any one side of the globe shows only part of Earth. Spin the globe to see a different part.

The **equator** is an imaginary line drawn around the center of the earth. People who live near the equator live in the warmest places on Earth. Can you find the equator on the globe? See Figure 1. The most northern point on Earth is called the **North Pole.** The most southern point on Earth is called the **South Pole.** Both of Earth's poles are very cold.

A globe is a model of Earth that is round like a ball.

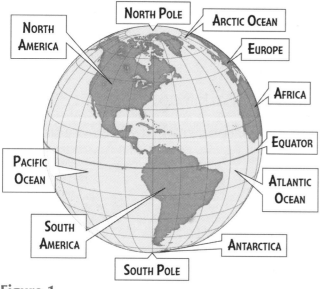

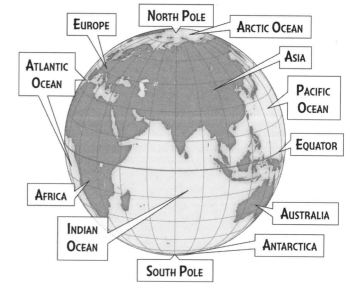

Figure 1

A globe is not the only model of Earth we use. Figure 2 is a flat model of Earth. It shows the entire Earth. It is called a **physical map.** A physical map shows Earth's different **landforms,** like deserts and mountains, or **water forms,** such as rivers and oceans.

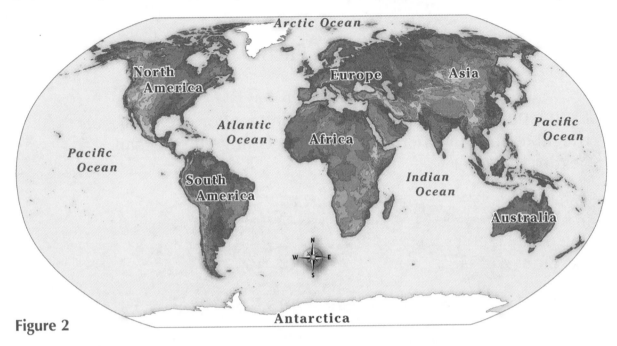

Figure 2

Maps and globes show that most of the earth is covered by water. The big areas of water, shown in blue, are called **oceans.** Can you find the four oceans on the physical map and the globe? The large areas of land are called **continents.** Earth's surface is divided into seven continents.

Some areas of land are shown in different colors on a physical map. These colors indicate the **elevation** of the land, or its height above sea level. The green areas are closer to sea level. The tan areas are higher and are often dry **prairies** or **deserts.** The darker brown areas show where mountains are on the continents. The white areas are the coldest areas on Earth.

The cross on the physical map is called a **compass rose.** You can use the directions on the compass rose to help describe where things are on the map. The four main directions are north (N), south (S), east (E), and west (W).

Build Your
Map Skills

Label a Physical Map of Earth

1. Each letter on the map indicates a continent or ocean. In the table below, write the name of the continent or ocean next to the letter.

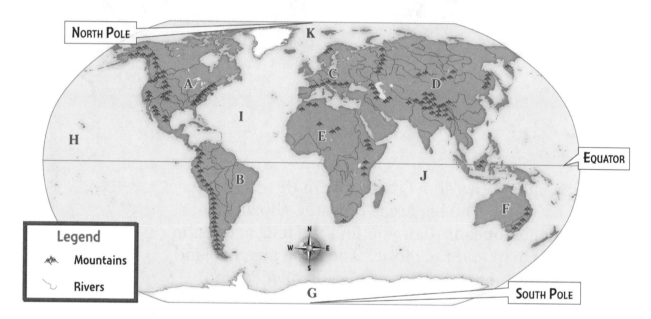

NORTH POLE

K

A   C   D

I

H   E

EQUATOR

B   J

F

Legend
🔺 Mountains
🌊 Rivers

N
W · E
S

G   SOUTH POLE

	Continent	Ocean
A		
B		
C		
D		
E		

	Continent	Ocean
F		
G		
H		
I		
J		
K		

Study the map to answer the following questions.

2. What is the largest ocean on Earth? _____

3. What is the smallest ocean on Earth? _____

4. What is the largest continent on Earth? _____

5. Which continent is also an island? _____

6. On which continent do you think the fewest people live?

   _____

   How does the map tell you that? _____

   _____

Use the compass rose on the map to help you answer these questions. Circle the correct answer.

7. Large mountains are found on the **east west** side of South America.

8. Europe is directly north of **Africa Asia.**

9. The Arctic Ocean is **north east** of North America.

10. Which continents does the equator touch? (There is more than one answer.)
    North America South America Africa Asia

Take the Animals Home

Something to Think About

How can a map help you travel over the world's oceans?

On pages 2 and 3, you learned about Earth's continents and oceans. In this lesson, you are the captain of a ship that is full of lost animals from all over the world. The animals want you to return them to their home continents.

Study the pictures in the table. Next to each picture, write the animal name and home continent that goes with the picture. (Use Appendix page 99 for help if you need it.)

Animal	Home Continent	Animal	Home Continent
giant panda	Asia		

Animal	Home Continent	Animal	Home Continent

Use the world map on page 4 to navigate the world's oceans to take the animals home. As you work through the questions, draw a line to each continent with a colored pencil.

1. From the star on the map, draw your route to Antarctica. Which animal will you take to Antarctica? penguin

   In which direction will you travel to get there? south

2. From Antarctica, draw your route to Africa.

   Which animals will you take to Africa? _____

   _____

   Through which ocean will you travel? _____

3. From Africa, draw your route to Asia.

   Which animals will you take to Asia? _____

   _____

   In which general direction will you travel to get there?

   _____

4. From Asia, draw your route to Australia.

   Which animals will you take to Australia? _____

   _____

   Through which ocean will you travel? _____

Your Place in the World

Where do you live? How would you answer that question? It might depend on who asked you.

Taylor Anderson has been thinking a lot lately about her place in the world. She started by asking herself the question, Where do I live? What do you think Taylor thought of first? She thought of her family and her own home. She smiled as she thought about curling up on the couch in the TV room, her favorite room of all. That's one place Taylor lives—one of her places in the world.

Taylor's home is just one place where she lives.

The next day at school, a classmate asked Taylor, "Where do you live?" How do you think Taylor answered? Do you think she said, "in my house"? No, this time Taylor replied with the name of her street. Her **neighborhood** is another one of Taylor's places in the world.

Taylor's neighborhood is also a place where she lives.

That weekend, her family took a short camping trip a couple hundred miles from their home. Taylor met another girl at the campground. Her new friend asked, "Where do you live?" This time, Taylor answered with the name of her town and **state.** She got a road map from her dad to show her new friend the location of Pine Lake, her **community.** She explained that her community is near the large city of Seattle.

Taylor thinks of the nearby city as also part of her home.

Taylor was soon able to think of still more answers to the question, "Where do you live?" For example, her state is located in a country, the United States of America. The United States is part of the continent of North America.

A **mental map** is a way of organizing information in your mind. When Taylor thought of her many places in the world, she used a mental map to help her. Like Taylor, you also have many different places in the world. You have a home, which is located on a particular street, which is in a community in your state, which is in the United States, which is in North America— which is on Earth! Did you realize you lived in so many different places?

Taylor Anderson's home in Pine Lake

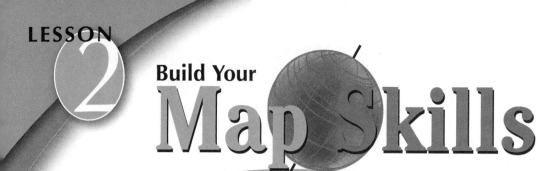

Build Your Map Skills

Follow Map Directions

You can use a map to help you find where things are and to get from place to place. Most maps include a compass rose and a legend, or map key.

A **legend** will show you what different symbols on a map mean. It is a small table that includes every symbol shown on a map. The legend describes the feature that each symbol or color stands for. If you are looking for a park on a map, for example, find the symbol in the legend that means *park*. Then, find that symbol on the map.

At the beginning of this lesson, you read about Taylor Anderson and her many places in the world. One of these places is the town of Pine Lake. Use this map of Pine Lake to answer the questions.

1. Follow the bike path to the school from Taylor's house. What important places does she pass?

   _____

2. Name two streets in Pine Lake that run north and south.

   _____

3. Which buildings are located on the corner of Main Street and Long Street? _____

4. Describe one route Taylor could use to walk to school each day. _____

   _____

5. Suppose Taylor is at Pine Lake Mall. What street is she on? _____

6. Describe a route she could take to get home from Pine Lake Mall. _____

_____

_____

_____

7. What is the name of the river that lies east of Taylor's house? _____

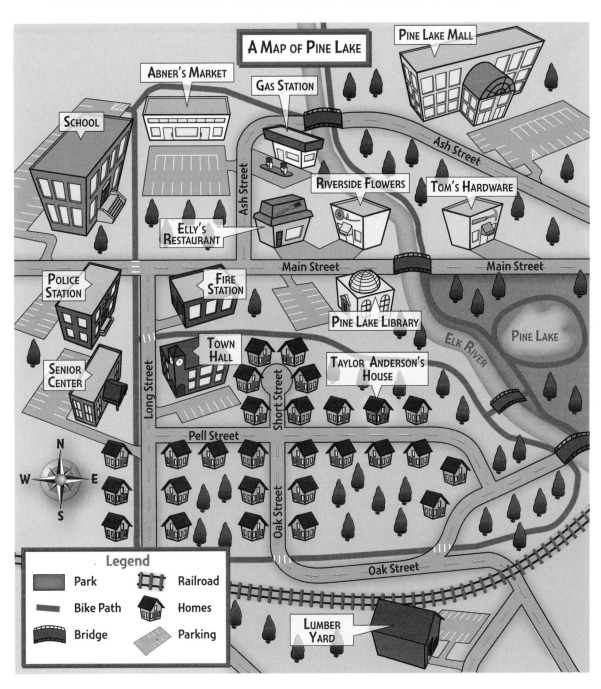

LESSON 2 Draw a Mental Map

How do people find their way when they go from place to place?

People often use a mental map to get from place to place. A mental map is your idea of where you are. A mental map should include buildings and places.

Think about the places you often go in your community. You may go to the post office to mail letters. You may go to the grocery store to buy food.

On pages 10 and 11, you worked with a simple map of Taylor Anderson's community. You learned how to locate important places and how to use a map to get from one place to another. In this activity, you will make a simple mental map of your own neighborhood or community.

1. Write your complete address, including your town or city, your state, and your ZIP code.

   _____

   _____

2. Make a list of some of the important places close to where you live (for example, your home, school, post office, grocery store, or friends' homes).

   _____

   _____

   _____

   _____

3. Are there any other important features near your home such as parks, lakes, or rivers?

_____

_____

4. What are the names of some important streets or highways in your community?

_____

_____

5. Think for a moment about the important places you named in question 2. Picture your home first. Then, think of where the other places are compared to where your home is located. On a separate piece of paper, draw a mental map of your neighborhood or community. Use the map of Pine Lake on page 11 as a model for your map.

6. Next to your map, make a simple legend, like the one on page 11.

7. Now, use the map you have created to plan a route from your home to a place in your community. Use the space below to describe your route. For example, your trip could be to school, to a park, or to a friend's house. Be sure to name the streets you need to use and the directions you need to travel to get where you are going.

When you finish, ask an adult to check your mental map and the route you planned. If you need to, walk through your neighborhood and make corrections.

_____

_____

_____

_____

_____

_____

_____

Understanding Maps

A **map** is a drawing of a part of Earth's surface as seen from above. It uses colors, symbols, and labels to represent features found on the ground. There are several different kinds of maps. (See Appendix page 100 to read about some of them.)

The kind of map you are probably most familiar with shows **locations,** or where things are. The map on the next page shows several locations within a town. Look at the map and study its many features.

A map's title tells you what the map is about. As you already know, a compass rose is a map symbol that shows directions. The four main directions (north, south, east, and west) are called **cardinal directions. Intermediate directions** on a compass rose are halfway between the cardinal directions. They are northwest (NW), southwest (SW), northeast (NE), and southeast (SE).

Symbols are drawings, lines, or dots that stand for something else. A map legend includes every symbol shown on a map and describes what each one stands for.

Notice the numbers and letters at the top and side of the map. **Gridlines** are the horizontal and vertical lines that extend from each number and letter. The place where two gridlines meet is a way to describe a place on the map. For example, the Pine Lake Senior Center is at location **G2.**

An **index** lists the names of places located on the map. Places listed in the index match up to a grid reference number, like F3, where two gridlines meet.

A map's **scale** shows the relationship between distance on the map and distance on the ground.

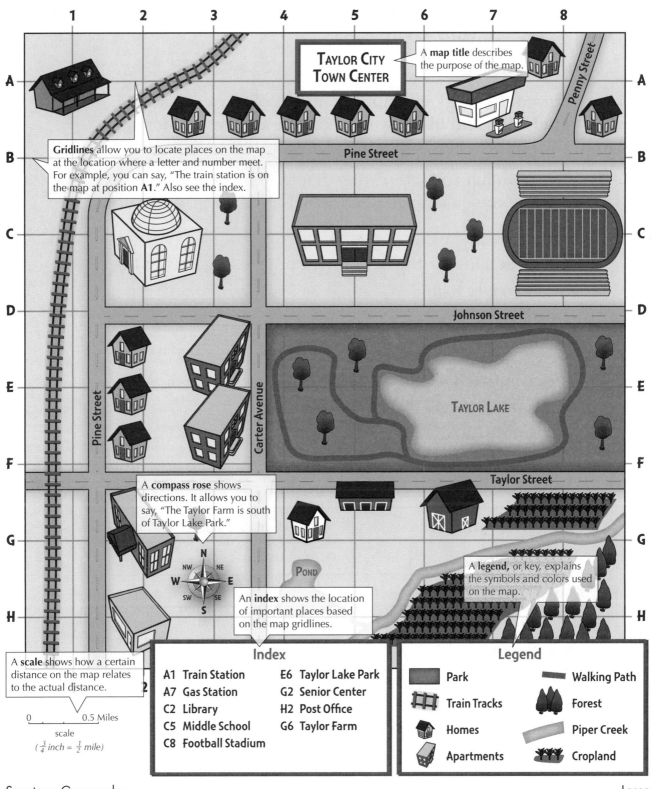

1 2 3 4 5 6 7 8

TAYLOR CITY TOWN CENTER

A **map title** describes the purpose of the map.

Gridlines allow you to locate places on the map at the location where a letter and number meet. For example, you can say, "The train station is on the map at position **A1**." Also see the index.

Pine Street

Johnson Street

TAYLOR LAKE

Taylor Street

A **compass rose** shows directions. It allows you to say, "The Taylor Farm is south of Taylor Lake Park."

N
NW NE
W E
SW SE
S

POND

A **legend,** or key, explains the symbols and colors used on the map.

An **index** shows the location of important places based on the map gridlines.

A **scale** shows how a certain distance on the map relates to the actual distance.

0   0.5 Miles
scale
($\frac{3}{4}$ inch = $\frac{1}{2}$ mile)

Index

A1	Train Station	E6	Taylor Lake Park
A7	Gas Station	G2	Senior Center
C2	Library	H2	Post Office
C5	Middle School	G6	Taylor Farm
C8	Football Stadium		

Legend

Park

Train Tracks

Homes

Apartments

Walking Path

Forest

Piper Creek

Cropland

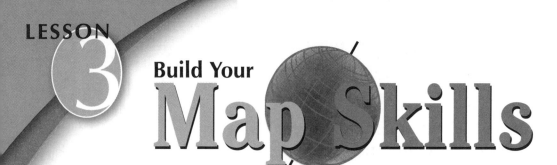

Build Your
Map Skills

Use a Map Grid

Your cousin Mark is visiting from out of town and wants you to help him find his way around. You will use this map of your town to help him locate the places he wants to visit.

1. Name two fun and interesting places Mark might like to visit that are on Orange Road. What are their grid locations?

   _____

2. Give directions for the best way for Mark to get from the library to city hall. _____

   _____

   _____

3. Mark wants to know if there are any parks in town. Are there? Name the park and its grid reference.

   _____

4. In the space below, create an index for this map. Each place in the index needs a grid reference number.

Map Index	Grid Number
Big Bay Harbor	
City Hall	
High School	
History Museum	
Library	
Post Office	
Shopping Mall	

5. From the park, Mark would like to ride his bike. Which direction does the bike path run? _____ The path runs along what creek? _____

6. Mark wants to mail some postcards to his friends back home. What is the grid reference for the post office? _____

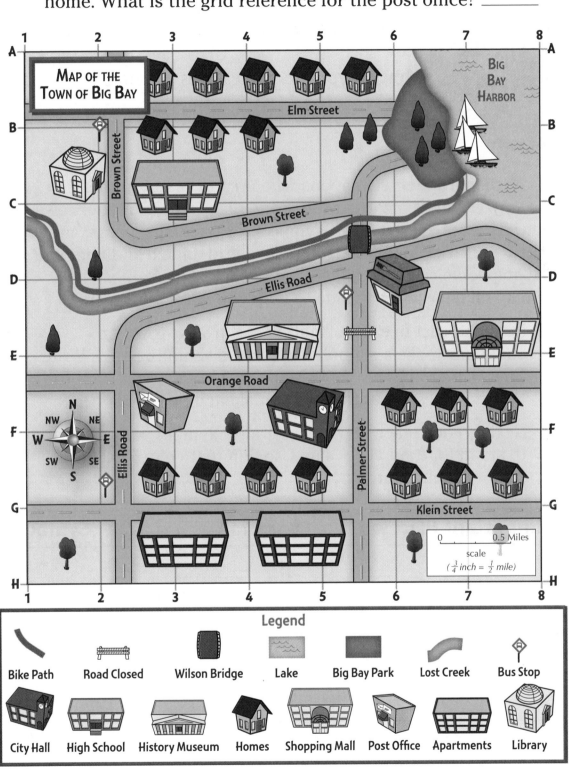

Make a Map with a Legend

Something to Think About

How do you use the features of a map?

A **cartographer** is someone who creates maps. In this lesson, you will be a cartographer and make a map of your town. You will create a legend with symbols for buildings, parks, and other landmarks. You will also create a grid, index, and compass rose so people can find things on the map easily. You can use the map on page 15 as a guide to help you make your map.

1. Name at least five important places in your town or community, like a school, a park, or a shopping mall. Write their names in the table below. Name more if you want to. Include notes about the location of each place.

2. Next to each place you listed, draw a symbol you will use to stand for it on your map. Use different colors for the symbols you create.

Important Places	Location	Symbol

3. Name at least five streets to include on your map. Next to each street name, write the direction it runs. Ask an adult for help with the directions if you are not sure.

Street Name	Direction

4. Now, get a large sheet of paper to draw your map. First, draw a compass rose in one of the corners. Then, draw lines on the map to show the streets you named in question 3. Draw the streets in the correct location and direction. Write the name of the streets on the map.

5. It is time to add the places you named in question 1 to the map. Use the symbols you created and put them on the correct streets.

6. Now, use a ruler to mark off gridlines on your map. Measure carefully to space the gridlines the same distance apart. Label the vertical gridlines with numbers at the top of your map. Label the horizontal gridlines with letters at the side of your map.

7. Create a map legend, using the symbols you created for the places on your map.

8. Finally, create a map index by listing the names and grid reference numbers of each place on your map.

What Makes a Community?

A community is a place where people live and work together. Some people live in large cities with thousands of other people. Some people live in small **towns.** Others live in **rural** or **suburban** areas. Appendix page 101 lists some different types of communities. How would you describe your community?

People decide to start communities in specific places for certain reasons. In the 1780s, southwest Ohio lay at the edge of the Northwest Territory. Few people lived there.

In 1788, a group of 47 pioneers arrived where the Muskingum and Ohio rivers come together. They began the community of Marietta, Ohio. The city's location on two major rivers helped Marietta become an important early center of **manufacturing.** People who work in manufacturing build things for people to buy. The rivers made it easier to ship products to customers.

Today, many people work hard in Marietta providing services to other people. A service is something that people do to benefit others. For example, local police officers help protect everyone who lives in Marietta. Teachers educate the community's children.

What service does this person provide to others?

The people of Marietta are proud of their city's history. Every year, they celebrate their history with festivals along the Muskingum and Ohio rivers. They remember how important the rivers were in the development of their community.

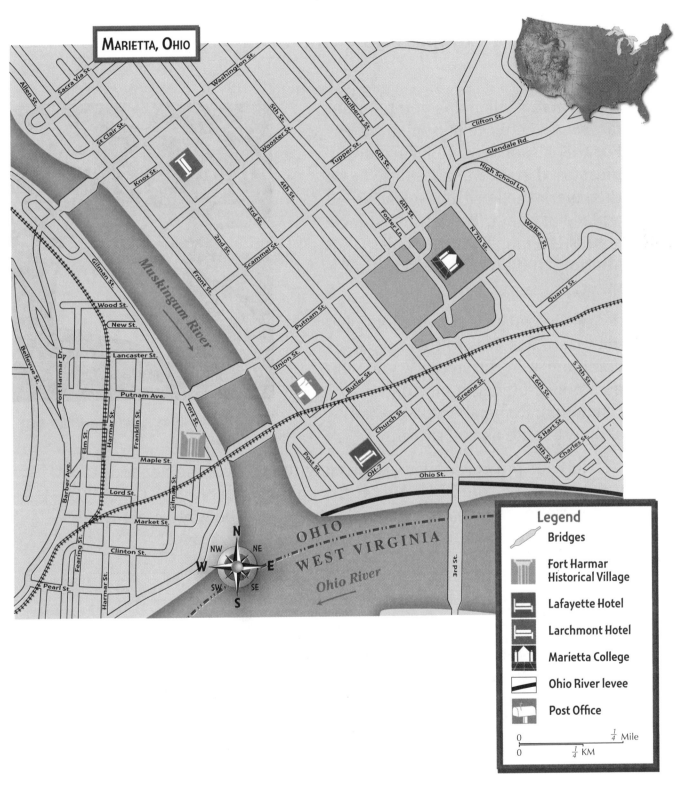

MARIETTA, OHIO

Legend

Bridges

Fort Harmar Historical Village

Lafayette Hotel

Larchmont Hotel

Marietta College

Ohio River levee

Post Office

0 — $\frac{1}{4}$ Mile

0 — $\frac{1}{4}$ KM

Build Your
Map Skills

Use a Compass Rose and Scale

A map scale helps you tell how far away one place is from another. For this lesson, you will learn how to measure distance in air miles. To do this, mark the length of the scale on a piece of paper. Track the distance across the map with the scale. Multiply to figure the distance in miles.

Police officers provide lots of important services to their community. In this activity, you will be a police officer in Lawton, Oklahoma. Remember to take the shortest route as you travel.

What things does a police officer do to help people?

1. In your police car, you are passing the golf course headed east on W Gore Blvd. A motorist on NW 38th St. near Greer Park needs help changing a flat tire. Describe how to get to the motorist. About how far will you need to travel?

_____

_____

_____

2. You get a call about a traffic accident at the corner of NW Cache Rd. and NW Sheridan Rd. Describe how you will get there from Greer Park.

_____

_____

3. You are at Comanche Hospital. There is a lost boy at Fred Bently Park who needs help getting home. About how far are you from this park? Which direction will you travel to get there?

_____

_____

_____

_____

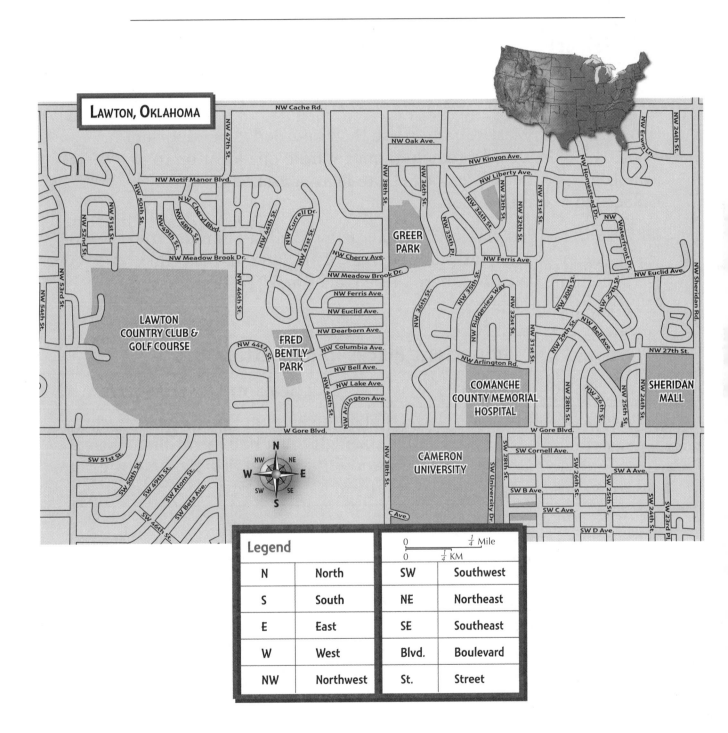

Legend		0 ____ ¼ Mile	
		0 ____ ¼ KM	
N	North	SW	Southwest
S	South	NE	Northeast
E	East	SE	Southeast
W	West	Blvd.	Boulevard
NW	Northwest	St.	Street

4 Locate Important Places

Why are certain places in your town important to you?

People in Marietta, Ohio, use their knowledge of important places and landmarks to help them get from one location to another. Use the map on page 21 to learn about important places in Marietta, Ohio.

1. In the left column of the table below is a list of important places or landmarks on the map of Marietta. In the right column, describe where these places are. The first item has been completed for you.

Important Places in Marietta, Ohio	
Important Places	**Location Description**
Muskingum River	The Muskingum River flows southeast through town between Gilman Street and Front Street. It flows into the Ohio River.
Fort Harmar Historical Village	
Post Office	
Marietta College	
Lafayette Hotel	

Refer to pages 20–21 and answer these questions about the community of Marietta, Ohio.

2. When was Marietta founded? Who founded the city?

_____

_____

_____

3. Why is Marietta's location on two rivers important to the community?

_____

_____

_____

4. There are many important places in your community. What do people at these places do for the community to make it better? Use the table below to describe important places in your community. Use a separate piece of paper, if necessary.

Important Places in Your Community	
Important Places	**Why Is This Place Important?**
Hospital	
Library	
School	
Police Station	
Other:	

What happens at a school that makes it an important place?

Communities within a State

The magnificent mountains of the Teton Range tower over the community of Jackson, Wyoming. The largest mountain in the range, the Grand Teton, is 13,770 feet high. Twelve other peaks are over 12,000 feet high. Rivers have cut deep valleys into the land, and many lakes lie at the foot of the range. With all this natural beauty, the people of Jackson enjoy lots of outdoor activities. Skiing, snowboarding, rock climbing, kayaking, and fishing are all popular. People come from all over the world to visit the Tetons and have rugged fun in the mountains.

The people who live in the Ozark region of northern Arkansas refer to the Ozarks as mountains, but the area is really a plateau. **Plateaus** are high, flat lands. People in the Ozarks say, "It's not that the mountains are so high, it's just that the valleys are so deep." The Boston Mountains are the tallest range within the Ozarks and reach as high as 2,570 feet. The valleys are between 500 to 1,550 feet deep. Fayetteville, home of the University of Arkansas, is the largest community in this part of the state. The eastern part of Arkansas is flat and fertile farmland. Many agricultural (farm) products like chickens, cattle, hogs, soybeans, and cotton are raised and grown here.

The Teton Range towers over Jackson, Wyoming.

Beautiful rivers flow through the Ozark Mountains.

Maine is known for its many pleasant, small communities.

Fewer people live in Maine than in any other state east of the Mississippi River. Called the *Pine Tree State,* 90 percent of the land is **forest.** Many forested parts of the state are almost uninhabited. The Northwest Aroostook territory in the far north has an area of 2,668 square miles and a population of only 27. That's only one person for every 100 square miles!

Maine's forested slopes sweep down to the Atlantic Ocean. Lighthouses, beaches, small fishing communities, and thousands of tiny islands are scattered along the state's rocky coastline. If you've ever eaten lobster, it probably came from Maine. The lumber and shipbuilding industries are also important in communities like Old Town, Maine.

Like Jackson, Fayetteville, and Old Town, all communities have different features depending on where they are located. How would you describe the physical features of your community?

Build Your
Map Skills

Use a State Map to Describe Communities

A map can help locate cities and features within a state. This map of Wyoming shows some of the larger communities and the state capital, Cheyenne. A state's **capital** is the city where the governor and elected officials meet to govern the state.

Mapmakers draw lines to show where states begin and end. These **boundaries** are imaginary lines that only exist on the map.

Many states have one or more national parks. A **national park** is an area of land set aside by an act of Congress because of its special value to all Americans. This map also shows physical features of the state of Wyoming, such as mountains, rivers, and lakes.

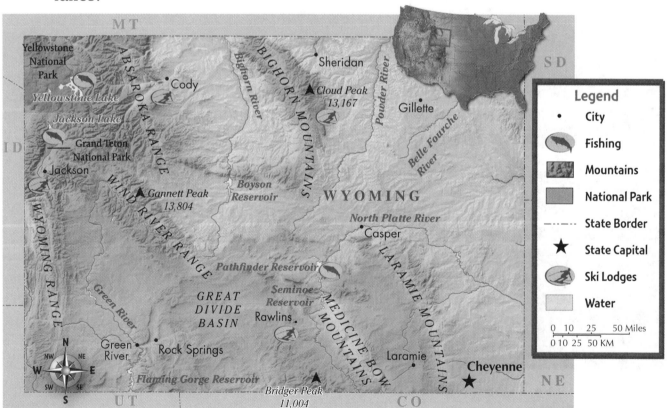

Answer the questions below to learn more about communities within the state of Wyoming.

1. In what part of the state is Wyoming's capital city located?

    _____

2. With which states does Wyoming share a border? (See Appendix page 98 for a key to state abbreviations.)

    _____

    _____

3. What are the names of the national parks shown on the map?

    _____

4. What is the name of the river that flows past Casper, Wyoming? _____

5. According to the map, near which cities is skiing popular?

    _____

6. Name two reservoirs shown on the map.

    _____

    _____

7. Look on Appendix page 101 for population information for the Wyoming communities shown on the map. List them below from the largest to the smallest based on their population. _____

    _____

The state government is located in Cheyenne, the capital.

LESSON 5

Make a State Vacation Guide

Something to Think About

Why are physical features of communities important?

In this activity, you will learn about the physical features of communities within a state. You will use facts about these places to create a vacation guide to attract people to visit there.

Refer again to pages 26–27, which describe both Arkansas and Maine. Study the maps of Arkansas and Maine on the next page. Choose one of these two states, and then answer the questions to help you plan your vacation guide. Use a separate piece of paper, if you need more room.

1. List some important physical features of the state you chose. You could include rivers, lakes, mountains, the coast, or other features in your list. _____

   _____

2. List things to do in the state that might be fun or educational for visitors. Make notes about why these activities would be fun or educational. _____

   _____

3. On a separate piece of paper, create a vacation guide for the state. Paste or tape pictures onto your vacation guide from magazines or newspapers. You should include at least one picture and a description of what makes the state a great place to visit. Use all the information you have put together to help create your vacation guide.

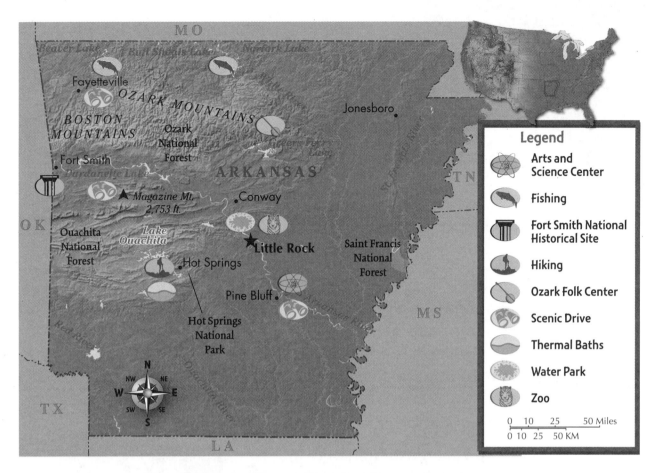

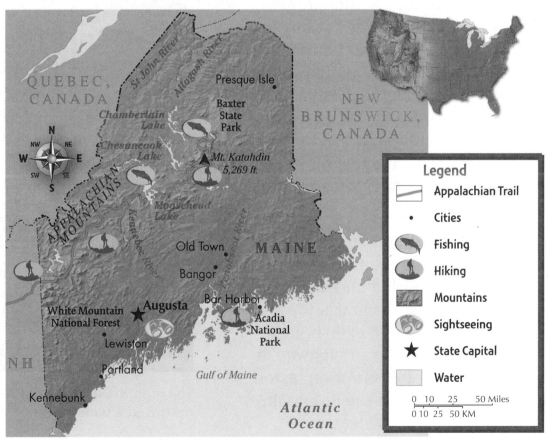

Landforms of the West

To a geographer, a landform refers to the shape, form, or nature of a specific physical feature of Earth's surface. Landforms are Earth's natural features. Hills, plains, and mountains are all examples of landforms. Some areas of the United States have different landforms than other areas. Many of the landforms of the American West are different than those found in the eastern parts of the country.

A **volcano** is an example of a landform. A volcano is a mountain where **magma** (molten rock) sometimes erupts through the earth's surface. Mount St. Helens is a famous volcano in the state of Washington. Early on May 18, 1980, Mount St. Helens **erupted** (exploded violently). Part of the mountain's north face was blown away. Dark ash fell all over the eastern part of the state.

During the Mount St. Helens eruption, a wide area of forest was blown down or buried under ashes and rocks. Thousands of animals were killed. The eruption destroyed 200 homes, 47 bridges, and 185 miles of highway. It killed 57 people. The eruption lasted 9 hours, and it reduced the mountain's height by almost 1,300 feet.

The eruption of Mount St. Helens destroyed a wide area of forest.

You may not believe it, but plant and animal life have returned to the area. Small plants began sprouting through the deposits of ash within months of the eruption. Many trees and shrubs have now made the area green again.

Another type of landform is called a **mesa**. A mesa is a high area of land with a flat top and sides that are usually steep cliffs. It looks something like a table rising from the flat, surrounding land. The Black Mesa in northeastern Arizona rises more than 1,000 feet above the surrounding grasslands. Native Americans from the Hopi and Navajo tribes have lived here for thousands of years.

Many springs in the southern areas of the mesa provide a dependable source of water. Native people have grown corn, squash, beans, and melons here for centuries.

Since the 1960s, the mesa has been strip-mined for coal. The mining has caused problems between the people who live on the mesa and the coal company, which uses the groundwater. Many native people consider the area sacred. They disapprove of coal being taken from the area.

Look at the table on page 34 and identify these landforms of the West.

Build Your Map Skills

Labeling Landforms and Water Forms

Look at the pictures and read the definitions of the different landforms below.

	butte A butte is an isolated hill with steep sides and a flat top. It is smaller than a mesa.		**mesa** A mesa is a high, wide area of land with a flat top and sides that are often steep cliffs. It is smaller than a plateau.
	canyon A canyon is a valley with steep, rocky sides. A river or creek often runs at the bottom of a canyon.		**mountain** A mountain is a rugged landform that rises much higher than the surrounding land.
	cliff A cliff is a steep, high face of rock.		**plateau** A plateau is a high flat area of land that is larger than a mesa.
	desert A desert is a large, dry region that receives little rain.		**river** A river is a large, natural stream of water that is larger than a creek.
	hill A hill is an elevated (raised) landform. It is smaller than a mountain, and its slopes are gentler.		**valley** A valley is a low-lying area of land, often containing a river and surrounded by higher areas such as mountains or hills.
	lake A lake is a water form that is surrounded by land.		**volcano** A volcano is a mountain or hill that usually contains molten rock and steam.

Identify the landforms and water forms on the map by writing their names in the blank spaces. When you are done, answer the questions below.

1. How are a plateau, a mesa, and a butte different from one another? _____

_____

_____

2. How are valleys and canyons the same? _____

_____

_____

3. How is a lake different than a river? _____

_____

_____

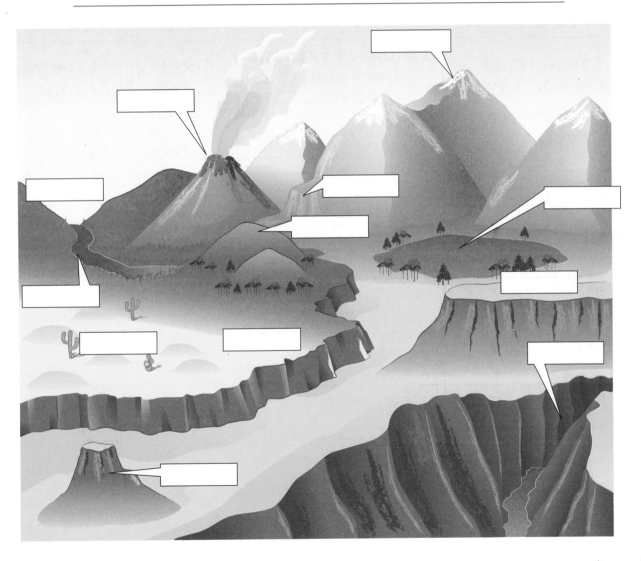

Landforms and Water Forms of Arizona

Why are landforms and water forms shown on a map?

Complete the table below by referring to the map of Arizona on page 37. The first item has been completed for you as an example.

Landform or Water Form Types	Landform Example from Map of Arizona	Location of Landform within Arizona
butte	Hopi Buttes	northeast of Winslow at the edge of the Painted Desert
canyon		
cliffs		
desert		
plateau		
river		
mesa		
mountains		

Answer the questions below.

1. What river runs through the city of Tucson? _____

_____

2. Which river runs near the city of Winslow? _____

_____

3. In what part of Arizona are most of the deep canyons and high mesas, buttes, and plateaus located?

_____

4. Bill Williams was a famous mountain man in the region. Describe the location of the river that was named for him.

_____

_____

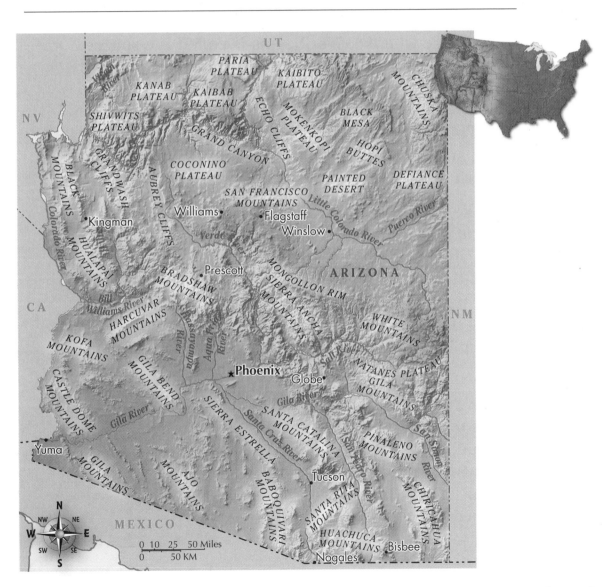

All about Lakes and Rivers

A **river** is a large stream of water that flows through the land. Smaller streams that join a bigger river are called **tributaries.** For example, the Tennessee River is a tributary of the Ohio River. It flows through Tennessee, Alabama, Mississippi, and Kentucky.

The place where a river begins is called the **source.** This is often a lake or spring where water flows out of the ground. The place where a river empties into a larger body of water is called the **mouth.** This larger body of water could be an ocean, a lake, or another river.

A **lake** is a body of water surrounded by land. Lakes can form naturally in many different ways. For example, the low areas where many lakes formed in the Upper Midwest were dug out by the movement of glaciers millions of years ago.

Lakes can also be made by people. A **reservoir** is a human-made lake. It is made by flooding land behind a **dam** (a barrier that holds back flowing water). For example, Watts Bar Lake in Tennessee is a reservoir created behind Watts Bar Dam.

A reservoir is a human-made lake.

Rivers and streams feed water into both natural lakes and reservoirs. This water from natural lakes, reservoirs, and rivers is used in many ways. It provides drinking water for people. It provides fish and many other animals with a place to live. Farmers use water from lakes and rivers to water their fields. Also, water from reservoirs is often used to make electricity.

People come to lakes and rivers to have fun in their spare time. This is called **recreation.** They fish, boat, water ski, and swim in lakes and rivers. In Tennessee, people having fun around the Tennessee reservoirs have created many businesses and jobs.

Rivers and lakes are also used to transport products important to the economy. For example, one reason the lakes on the Tennessee River were created was for **navigation,** or the transportation of materials and products with ships. The deep water in the lakes is needed for large ships full of heavy material such as coal.

Barges are large ships that carry materials, such as gravel, grain, coal, and lumber. They are a good way to transport material because one barge can sometimes hold as much as 60 large trucks. A **port** is a place located on a river or lake that can receive barges and transfer cargo to and from them.

Barges transport materials, such as gravel, grain, coal, and lumber.

Build Your

Reading a River Map

Look at the map and read again about the Tennessee River on pages 38–39. Then, answer the questions below.

1. The Tennessee River officially begins one mile above Knoxville, Tennessee. Name the states through which the Tennessee River flows. _____

   _____

2. Complete the table below about the lakes on the Tennessee River. (Two of the lakes extend into more than one state.)

Dam	Name of Lake	States
Pickwick Dam	Pickwick Lake	Alabama, Mississippi, and Tennessee

3. Name the three main tributary rivers on the map that flow into the Tennessee River. _____

_____

4. What other large river system flows from east to west across Tennessee and empties into the Ohio River near Paducah, Kentucky? _____

5. Where is the mouth of the Tennessee River?

_____

_____

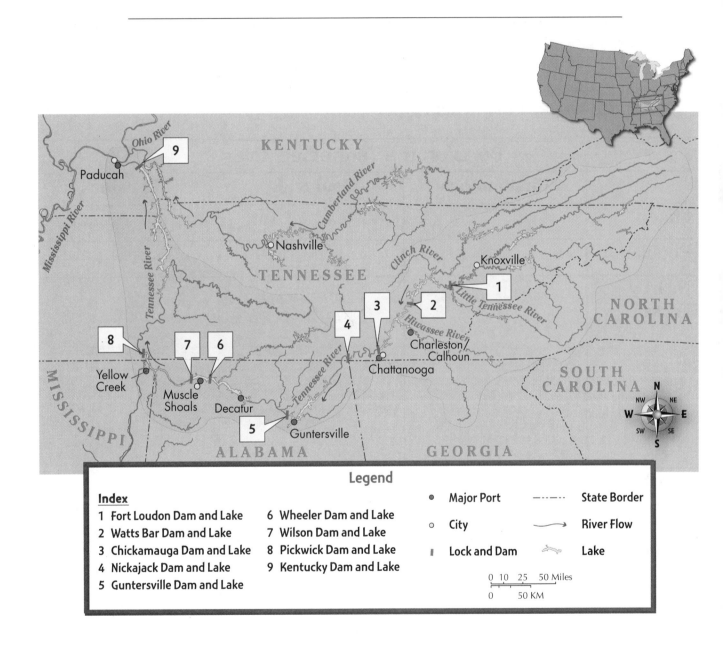

Legend

Index
1 Fort Loudon Dam and Lake
2 Watts Bar Dam and Lake
3 Chickamauga Dam and Lake
4 Nickajack Dam and Lake
5 Guntersville Dam and Lake

6 Wheeler Dam and Lake
7 Wilson Dam and Lake
8 Pickwick Dam and Lake
9 Kentucky Dam and Lake

● Major Port
○ City
▮ Lock and Dam

------- State Border
→ River Flow
Lake

0 10 25 50 Miles
0 50 KM

Learn about River Communities

Something to Think About

What is unique about river communities?

Complete the tables. Use the information on page 41 and on Appendix page 105 to help you.

Ports on the Tennessee River			
	Chattanooga	**Paducah**	**Decatur**
State			
Population			
Nearby Parks			
Nearby Reservoirs			
Museums			

Reservoirs on the Tennessee River				
	Kentucky	**Nickajack**	**Pickwick**	**Watts Bar**
Length of shoreline (miles)				
Size (acres)				
Year completed				

Use information from pages 38–39 to answer the following questions.

1. What is a port? _____

_____

_____

2. What is a reservoir? _____

_____

3. Name one way that water is used from the reservoirs on the Tennessee River. _____

4. What is the difference between a river's source and a river's mouth? _____

_____

_____

5. Why is recreation important to businesses in Tennessee?

_____

_____

6. Refer to the list of rivers on Appendix page 104. What are the four longest rivers in the United States? _____

_____

_____

7. How long is the Tennessee River? _____

_____

Where Early Native Americans Lived

The lives of the first Americans depended a lot on where they lived. Native Americans adapted to their environments. This means that the way they lived depended on the natural resources around them. **Natural resources** are things that occur in nature that are useful to human beings, such as water, plants, and wildlife.

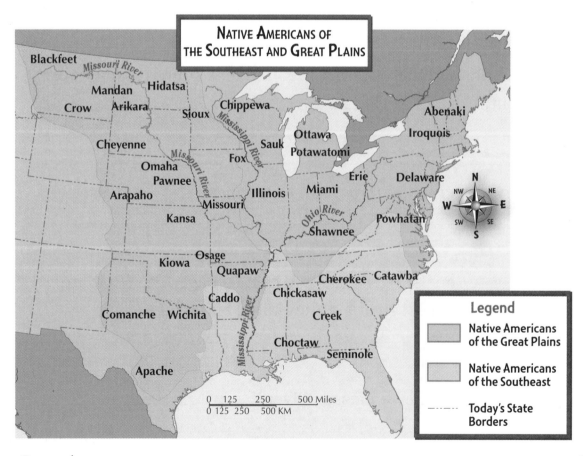

NATIVE AMERICANS OF THE SOUTHEAST AND GREAT PLAINS

Blackfeet
Missouri River
Mandan   Hidatsa
Crow   Arikara
Sioux
Chippewa
Abenaki
Cheyenne
Ottawa
Sauk   Potawatomi
Iroquois
Fox
Omaha
Missouri River
Pawnee
Erie   Delaware
Arapaho
Illinois   Miami
Missouri
Ohio River
Kansas
Powhatan
Shawnee
Osage
Kiowa
Quapaw
Cherokee   Catawba
Chickasaw
Caddo
Comanche   Wichita
Creek
Choctaw
Seminole
Mississippi River
Apache

0   125   250   500 Miles
0 125 250   500 KM

Legend

Native Americans of the Great Plains

Native Americans of the Southeast

Today's State Borders

The Great Plains lie between the Rocky Mountains and the Mississippi River. This region is flat and dry. Winters are cold. Before white settlers came, millions of bison lived on the grasslands there. Native Americans, such as the Sioux, depended upon the bison. The Sioux lived in the area that is now Minnesota and North and South Dakota.

The Sioux lived a **nomadic** life. This means that they did not live in one place all the time. They hunted bison, following the herds as they wandered across the plains. The bison gave the Sioux everything they needed to survive. Bison meat provided them with food. They made clothing from bison skins. They even made tools from bison bones. The Sioux honored the spirit of the bison and other animals.

Because they followed the bison, the Sioux made houses called *tipis* out of bison hides that were light and easy to take apart and put back together.

Before white settlers moved onto their lands, the Cherokee, another Native American tribe, lived in a wide area of the southeast United States. Over time, the area where they lived became smaller due to white settlement.

The Cherokee lived different lives than the Sioux. The southeast is not dry like the Great Plains. The seasons are mild and there is plenty of rain. Because the land is good for farming, the Cherokee were farmers. They grew corn, squash, beans, and sunflowers. They also hunted deer, turkey, and other game and fished in nearby rivers.

Because they could survive by farming, the Cherokee were not nomadic. They lived in settled villages of houses, which were often built with thatched roofs of plant stalks or bark. They made clothing from deerskins. The Cherokee were known for their pipe carving, baskets, gourd art, and pottery.

The Sioux followed the bison.

The Sioux of the Great Plains lived in tipis.

The Cherokee grew crops such as corn, beans, and sunflowers.

Build Your Map Skills

Use a Map to Learn about the Movement of People

The Cherokee, Chickasaw, Choctaw, Creek, and Seminole are Native American tribes that originally lived in the southeastern United States. As the white population grew in the early 1800s, white settlers and Native Americans fought over control of the land.

In 1829, white people looking for gold entered land where the Cherokee people lived. This created problems between the Cherokee and the whites. The government forced the Cherokee to move to Indian Territory (Oklahoma).

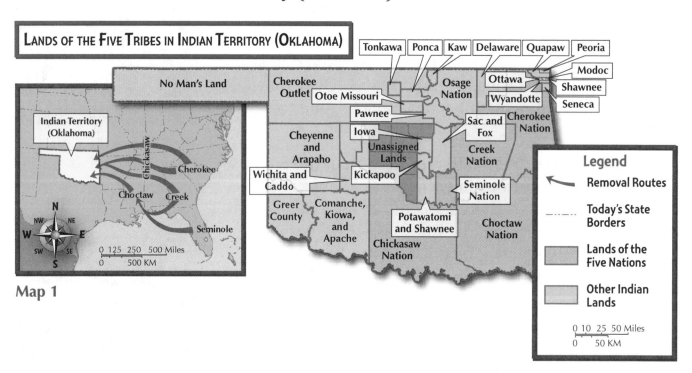

Map 1

Their journey west became known as the *Trail of Tears*. The Cherokee were divided into a number of groups. Some groups traveled by river to Indian Territory. The rest went overland on existing roads, taking many routes. The Northern Route was used most often.

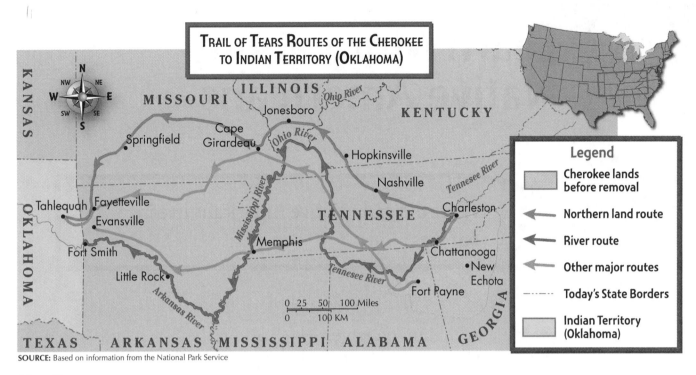

TRAIL OF TEARS ROUTES OF THE CHEROKEE TO INDIAN TERRITORY (OKLAHOMA)

Legend
- Cherokee lands before removal
- ← Northern land route
- ← River route
- ← Other major routes
- ‒·‒·‒ Today's State Borders
- Indian Territory (Oklahoma)

SOURCE: Based on information from the National Park Service

Map 2

Use the maps to answer the following questions.

1. Refer to Map 1. What are the names of the Five Nations that were removed from their lands in the southeast United States? _____

   _____

2. Refer to Map 2. Where did the Northern Route begin and end? _____

   _____

3. Refer to Map 2. Over what rivers and through what states did the Cherokee travel when following the river route? Write your answers in the table below.

Rivers	States
Tennessee River	Tennessee, Alabama, Mississippi, and Kentucky

Learn More about Native Americans

Something to **Think** About

Where did early Native Americans live in your area?

1. Review the information on pages 44–45 about the Sioux and Cherokee. Use the information on those pages to fill in the table below.

	Sioux	Cherokee
In what area of North America did they live before the white settlers came?		
What is the land and weather like where they originally lived?		
What kinds of foods did they eat?		
What kinds of houses did they live in?		
What kind of clothes did they wear?		

For the next activity, you will do some research in the library or in books you may have. If you need to, ask an adult for help finding some of the information.

2. Find out about the lives of the Sioux and Cherokee people today. Use the information you find to fill in the table.

	Sioux	Cherokee
Where do they live today?		
What kinds of jobs do they have today?		
What kinds of houses do they live in today?		

3. Find out about a Native American community in or near your state. Write what you learn in the table.

What is the name of the Native American community?	
Where did these people live in the past? Where do they live today?	
How did they use the land in the past? What kinds of jobs do they have today?	

Founding the Plymouth Colony

A **colony** is a community of people who settle far from their home but stay in touch with their homeland. Plymouth Colony, in Massachusetts, was one of the first permanent European settlements in America. Plymouth Colony was settled by the **Pilgrims** who came from England.

The Pilgrims' religious beliefs were different from those of most of the people in England. They wanted to live in a place where they could worship the way they liked. They decided to move to America. So in September 1620, 102 passengers plus crew boarded the ship *Mayflower,* hoping to reach present-day Virginia. However, the *Mayflower* was forced off course. The Pilgrims finally landed at the site of present-day Plymouth, Massachusetts, on December 21, 1620.

The voyage of the *Mayflower* across the Atlantic Ocean took 65 days.

Almost half of the Pilgrims died during their first winter at Plymouth Colony. Survival was difficult in the early years, but the Pilgrims made friends with nearby Wampanoag Indians—like Squanto and Chief Massasoit. They showed the Pilgrims how to gather seafood, trap beaver, and grow corn. After the first harvest in the fall of 1621, the settlers invited the Wampanoag to celebrate a harvest feast. The Pilgrims had learned how to survive by using the natural resources around them, such as the land, forests, and ocean.

Plymouth remained a small colony, growing very slowly. That did not bother the Pilgrims, though. They just wanted to live quietly and simply according to their religious beliefs. However, other settlers also arrived in America hoping for a new life. Eventually, settlements like the one at Plymouth expanded into 13 colonies along the Atlantic coast.

Some of the early American colonies are shown on the historical map. A **historical map** does not show places as they are now. It shows the way places were in the past. Historical maps help us better understand the way things used to be.

The Pilgrims made friends with nearby Indians.

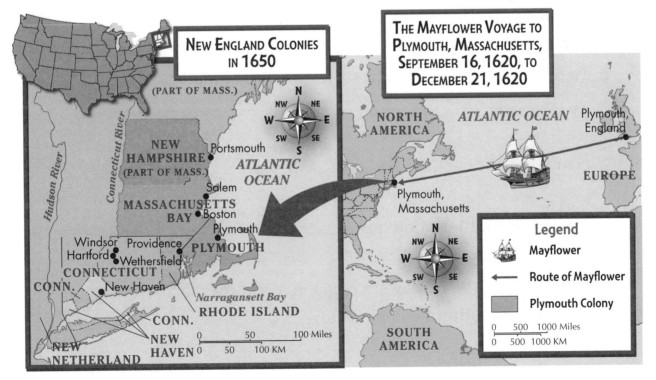

NEW ENGLAND COLONIES IN 1650

THE MAYFLOWER VOYAGE TO PLYMOUTH, MASSACHUSETTS, SEPTEMBER 16, 1620, TO DECEMBER 21, 1620

Legend
- Mayflower
- Route of Mayflower
- Plymouth Colony

0   500   1000 Miles
0   500   1000 KM

Build Your Map Skills

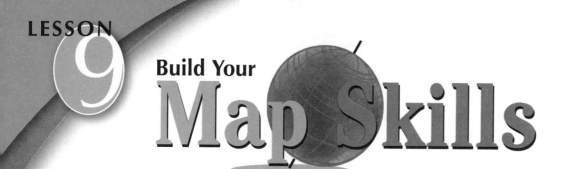

Learn about the Economy of the 13 Colonies

The business and work done by people in a community is called an **economy.** Natural resources are very important to most economies. For example, wood from trees is a natural resource. People in the American Colonies used wood to make tables and chairs. They then sold the tables and chairs to other people in the community.

The people of Plymouth Colony learned how to use the natural resources around them in order to live. Other settlers who formed colonies in America also used natural resources in their economies. Different colonies became good at making and growing different things. They traded and sold these products to make money.

The map shows some of the products made and sold by the 13 colonies. Look at the map and answer the following questions.

1. Name the Northern Colonies shown on the map.

   _____

   _____

2. Name the Middle Colonies. _____

   _____

3. Name the Southern Colonies. _____

   _____

4. According to the map, were ships made in the Northern, Middle, or Southern colonies? _____

   _____

5. In which colonies was tobacco grown? _____

_____

_____

6. What products were produced in South Carolina and Georgia that were not produced in the Northern Colonies?

_____

7. In which colonies was trapping important? _____

_____

_____

8. Name three colonies that probably had large forests. How do you know? _____

_____

_____

_____

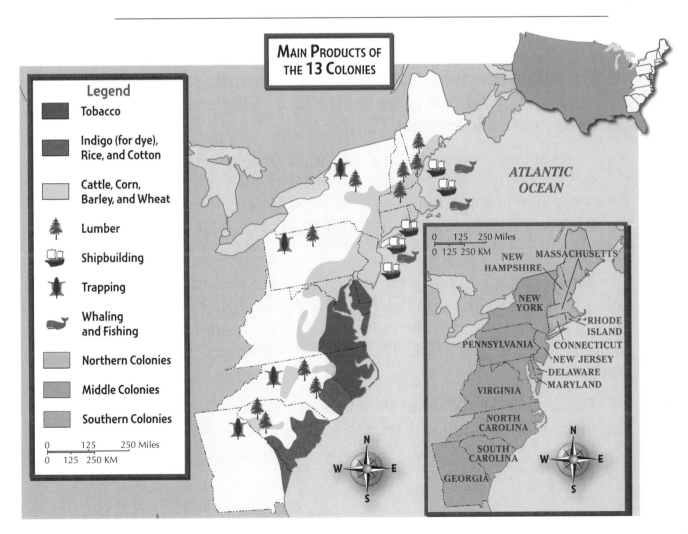

MAIN PRODUCTS OF THE 13 COLONIES

Legend
- Tobacco
- Indigo (for dye), Rice, and Cotton
- Cattle, Corn, Barley, and Wheat
- Lumber
- Shipbuilding
- Trapping
- Whaling and Fishing
- Northern Colonies
- Middle Colonies
- Southern Colonies

0   125   250 Miles
0   125   250 KM

ATLANTIC OCEAN

0   125   250 Miles
0   125 250 KM

NEW HAMPSHIRE   MASSACHUSETTS
NEW YORK
RHODE ISLAND
PENNSYLVANIA   CONNECTICUT
NEW JERSEY
DELAWARE
MARYLAND
VIRGINIA
NORTH CAROLINA
SOUTH CAROLINA
GEORGIA

The Economy Where You Live

What do people do in your community to make a living?

In this lesson, you have learned how early American colonists used resources. Today, communities still use resources. The workers who use resources to make goods or provide services are called **producers.**

There are three types of resources: natural, human, and capital. You have already learned about natural resources. **Human resources** are the people who do the work, sometimes called *labor*. **Capital resources** are the tools people use to make goods or to provide services.

A **good** is a product that people want or need. Goods are things you can touch, like a car that you ride in or the food you eat. A **service** is something that one person does for another person. For example, a person who delivers the mail is providing a service.

When painters paint your house, they are providing a service. The work they do is labor. Their paint brushes are their capital resources. When the painters are done, your family pays them money for their work. That's how the painters "make a living."

Confusing? Think about the kinds of work people do in your community. Then, it all will start to make more sense.

Picture 1

Picture 2

Picture 3

1. Look at Picture 1, which shows a painter painting a house. Who is the producer in the picture? What tools does he use to do the job? _____

   _____

   Is the painter providing a good or a service?

   _____

2. Look at Picture 2. Is the barber making a good or providing a service for the boy? What tools does he use?

   _____

   _____

3. Look at Picture 3, which shows a worker building a car. Is this worker making a good or providing a service?

   _____

4. In the table, write the names of two adults you know and the work they do to make a living. Write whether they produce mostly goods or services.

Names of Adults	What They Do	Goods or Services?

Farms and Farmers

Do you live in a city? If so, what comes to mind when you think of a farm? You may think that farms and farmers have little to do with your life. But agriculture is important to everyone.

Agriculture is the work of raising crops and livestock (farm animals). Agriculture produces our food and many other products we use all the time. Growing crops and raising animals is not all there is to agriculture. Sometimes, these farm products must be processed, or turned into other products, before we can use them.

There are more than two million farms all across the United States. Some parts of the country are better for growing and raising a certain kind of farm product. For example, many fresh fruits and vegetables are grown in warm areas like Florida, Texas, and California. The growing season is longer in these areas of the country. Many grains, like wheat and corn, grow well in Midwestern and Plains states, such as Nebraska and Kansas. Idaho is famous for its potatoes for a reason: potatoes grow best where it is cool. Other parts of the United States are not very good for growing crops, but they provide good grasslands for raising livestock.

Farmers milk their cows, and then they send the milk to a factory to be processed.

To understand agriculture, think about two different kinds of farm products and what happens to them before they reach our stores.

Much of the flour used to bake bread, cookies, and cake comes from wheat. After the wheat has been planted and grown, it is **harvested,** or gathered from the fields. After the harvest, the wheat is transported to a place where it is stored for future use. The grains of wheat are cleaned and then broken into smaller bits. These bits are rolled and sifted over and over until they become flour.

Much of the milk drank by human beings comes from cows. The cows turn the food they eat into milk. Farmers milk their cows, and the milk is stored in a large, cold tank where it stays fresh until it is picked up and taken to a factory. At the factory, the milk is heated to kill any germs it may have. Finally, the milk is put into bottles or cartons and delivered to stores for you to buy.

A factory may make cheese, butter, or other products from milk.

Build Your
Map Skills

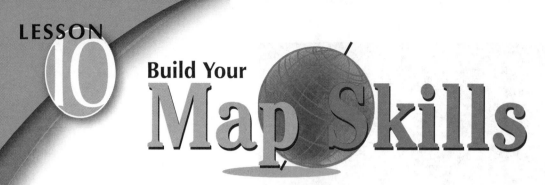

Use an Agricultural Map

As you have already learned, farm crops are grown and animals are raised on farms all over the United States. The type of farm products that can be produced in each area of the country depends upon the weather, rainfall, and type of soil in that area.

An **agricultural map** gives information related to farms and farming. For example, it can show the number of farms in a state or the type of crops that farmers grow. Map 1 shows the number of milk cows in each state in the United States. Map 2 shows the number of milk cows in each county of the state of Pennsylvania. (A county is a local area within a state.)

Use Map 1 to answer the following questions.

1. Which five states have the most milk cows?

_____

_____

2. According to Map 1, most states have about how many milk cows?

_____

3. Which state has more milk cows, California or Minnesota?

_____

Use Map 2 to answer the following questions.

4. Which five counties in Pennsylvania have the most milk cows? What cities and towns are located in those counties? Write this information in the table.

County	Cities and Towns

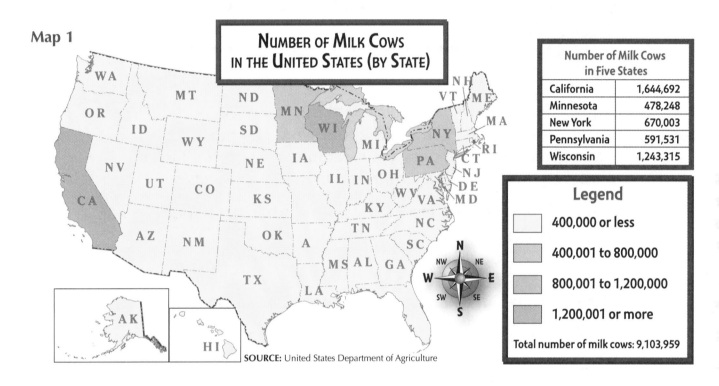

Map 1

NUMBER OF MILK COWS IN THE UNITED STATES (BY STATE)

Number of Milk Cows in Five States	
California	1,644,692
Minnesota	478,248
New York	670,003
Pennsylvania	591,531
Wisconsin	1,243,315

Legend

- 400,000 or less
- 400,001 to 800,000
- 800,001 to 1,200,000
- 1,200,001 or more

Total number of milk cows: 9,103,959

SOURCE: United States Department of Agriculture

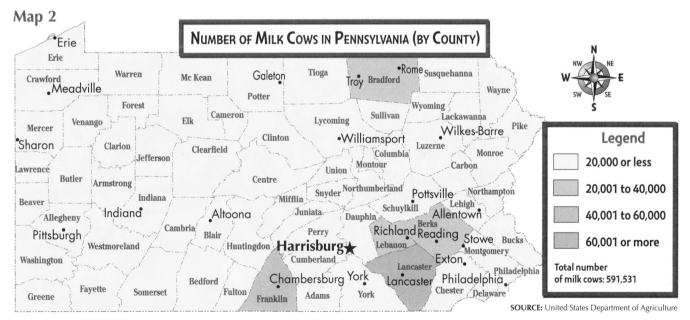

Map 2

NUMBER OF MILK COWS IN PENNSYLVANIA (BY COUNTY)

Legend

- 20,000 or less
- 20,001 to 40,000
- 40,001 to 60,000
- 60,001 or more

Total number of milk cows: 591,531

SOURCE: United States Department of Agriculture

LESSON 10

Agriculture in Your State

Something to Think About

Why are farms and farmers important?

In this lesson, you have learned about many types of farm products. Have you ever thought about what farm products might be grown or made near your community? Do the farms near where you live produce different kinds of products?

1. What farm crops are grown in your state or near your community? _____

_____

2. What farm animals are raised in your state or near your community? _____

_____

3. Visit a local grocery store and ask to talk to the store manager. Ask if the store sells any farm products that are grown or raised locally. If so, list them. _____

_____

_____

Find out how farm life has changed over the past 50 years. Talk to relatives or neighbors who grew up on farms. Ask them the following questions, and write down the answers.

4. Where was the farm where you grew up? _____

_____

_____

5. What was farm life like? How was it different than your life now? _____

_____

_____

6. What farm products did your farm produce? _____

_____

_____

7. List two of your favorite foods in the table below. Find out where these foods come from—do they come from a plant or an animal? How are they grown or made?

Favorite Food	Where is it grown or made? How is it processed?

Wool is from the outer coat of sheep. It is processed and dyed (colored) to make yarn and other products.

The Ways We Travel

How do you get from one place to another? Maybe you walk to a friend's house or ride in a bus or car to school. Maybe you have even flown on an airplane, if you were going somewhere far away.

The word **transportation** refers to the many ways of moving people and things from place to place. Bikes, cars, trucks, buses, trains, planes, and ships are all common methods of transportation. The pictures on these pages show some different methods of transportation.

Can you think of some of the reasons why people travel from place to place? When you need to buy a new pair of jeans or visit the doctor, transportation gets you where you need to go. People also need to get to their jobs every day. They may ride the bus, drive their cars, or take a train. Some people ride their bikes to work. Some even walk.

What are some of the reasons people travel from place to place?

The products you use every day have to be transported to the store where you go to buy them. As you have already learned, food grown on farms is often transported to factories to be processed. Packages of food are then brought to stores. Things such as clothes, computers, and furniture must be moved from where they are made to you.

Many of the things in your home were probably made in other countries, like Germany or China. How do you think they got to you? A cargo ship probably carried them across the ocean to a port city in the United States. The products were then unloaded and placed on a truck to be delivered to a store in your community. By the time products reach the store, they may have been transported in many different ways.

These Amish people travel by horse and buggy.

A cargo ship carries products across the ocean.

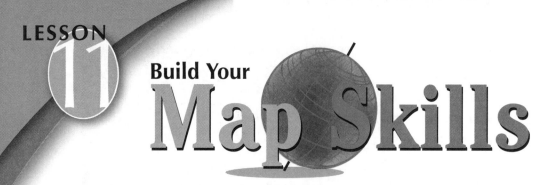

Build Your Map Skills

Use a County Road Map

The map on the next page shows Laurens County in the state of South Carolina. A **county** is a local area with political boundaries within a state. Most states have many counties.

The **interstate highways** shown on the map are part of a larger network of roads connecting cities and states all over the country. They may have two, three, or even four lanes going both ways. There are no traffic lights on interstate highways.

U.S. highways are usually smaller than interstate highways. They are more often two-lane roads. These highways also allow travel from one state to another. A **state** or **county** road is usually a two-lane road.

Use the map to answer the questions below.

1. Start at the far western corner of the county (near Princeton). From there, measure to the far eastern corner of the county. About how far is it? Use the map scale. Write the distance below.

   _____

2. Start at the northwest corner of Laurens County (north of Fountain Inn). Measure to the southeast corner of the county (southeast of Cross Hill). About how far is it? Write the distance below.

   _____

3. Name two interstate highways that run through Laurens County. In what direction do they run?

   _____

   _____

4. Describe what roads you would use to get from Gray Court to Princeton. Use the compass rose to describe the directions you would travel.

_____

_____

_____

5. Describe how you would travel from the town of Clinton to Cross Hill.

_____

_____

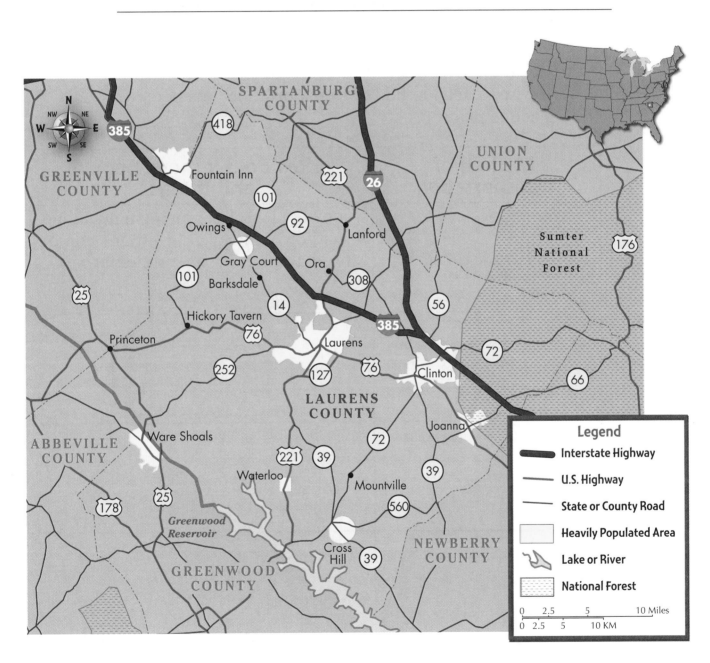

Transportation in Your Town

What is so important about the transportation of people and things?

1. Write down three methods of transportation in your town. Describe how each method of transportation gets people from place to place.

Method of transportation	How does it move people and things?
bicycle	It moves mostly people, usually along a road or pathway. A few items can be stored in a basket or saddle bags.

2. Ask three adults how they get to work each day. What type of transportation do they use? What route do they take to get to work? Write your answers below.

Name	Type of Transportation	Route to Work
Jason	Bus	north on the circle freeway

3. Using magazines and newspapers, find some pictures of products being transported in several different ways. These methods of transportation could be by train, in trucks or cars, on ships, or any other method of transportation. Cut the pictures out and tape them on a separate piece of paper. Now use the pictures to make up a story about transportation. Your story should answer as many of the questions below as possible. Add any other details that you think are important. Write your story on a separate piece of paper.

What items are being transported? _____

Where did the items come from? _____

Where are the items going? _____

How will the items be used? _____

The Need for Clean Water

Nature uses water over and over. Water keeps moving around in a natural process called the **water cycle.** Here's how the water cycle works.

You probably see water every day in its liquid form in oceans, rivers, and lakes. When the sun shines on the water, the water turns into water vapor. This water vapor rises above the earth and into the atmosphere. This process is called **evaporation.**

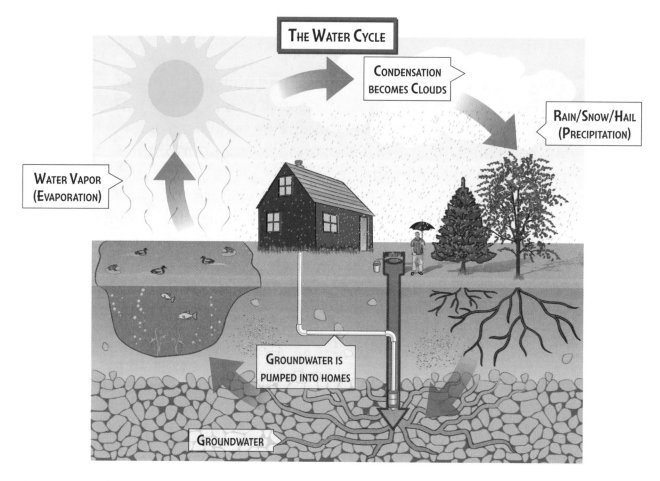

THE WATER CYCLE

CONDENSATION BECOMES CLOUDS

RAIN/SNOW/HAIL (PRECIPITATION)

WATER VAPOR (EVAPORATION)

GROUNDWATER IS PUMPED INTO HOMES

GROUNDWATER

As more and more water vapor rises above Earth, it **condenses** to form clouds. From the clouds, **precipitation** then falls to Earth as rain. Rain is water in liquid form again. Precipitation may also fall to Earth as snow or hail (water in solid form). The precipitation flows into oceans, rivers, and lakes, and the water cycle begins again.

We need drinking water to live. Plants and animals need water to live, too. It's important for us to keep our water as clean as possible so we can drink it.

Frogs live in wetlands within weed beds.

Water that has become spoiled in some way is said to be **polluted.** There are many ways that people pollute water. Sometimes, factories pollute water by dumping chemicals into oceans, rivers, and lakes.

Wetlands are natural areas that are often wet or flooded. They work as nature's water filter. Wetlands can remove some types of pollution from the water we drink and use every day. But often wetlands are drained to make farmland or for land to build houses or shopping malls. When this happens, nature's important water filter is lost.

Ducks live in all types of wetlands.

Otters eat fish. They live in dens along rivers and lakes.

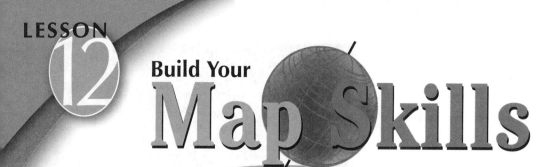

Build Your

Map Skills

Reading a Precipitation Map

Different parts of the United States get different amounts of precipitation. Map 1 shows the precipitation received throughout the United States over one year. Map 2 shows the precipitation that falls each year in North Dakota. The amounts on the map are average amounts. That means it rains or snows about that much every year.

Study the maps and answer the following questions.

1. Look at Map 1. Which states in the West get the most precipitation? Write the state names in the space below.

_____

2. On Map 1, which states do you think include desert regions? How do you know? _____

_____

_____

3. Study Map 2 and complete the table below.

Cities and Counties in North Dakota	Location within the State	Average Annual Precipitation
Bismarck	Burleigh County	15–20 inches
Bowman County		
Fargo		
Griggs County		

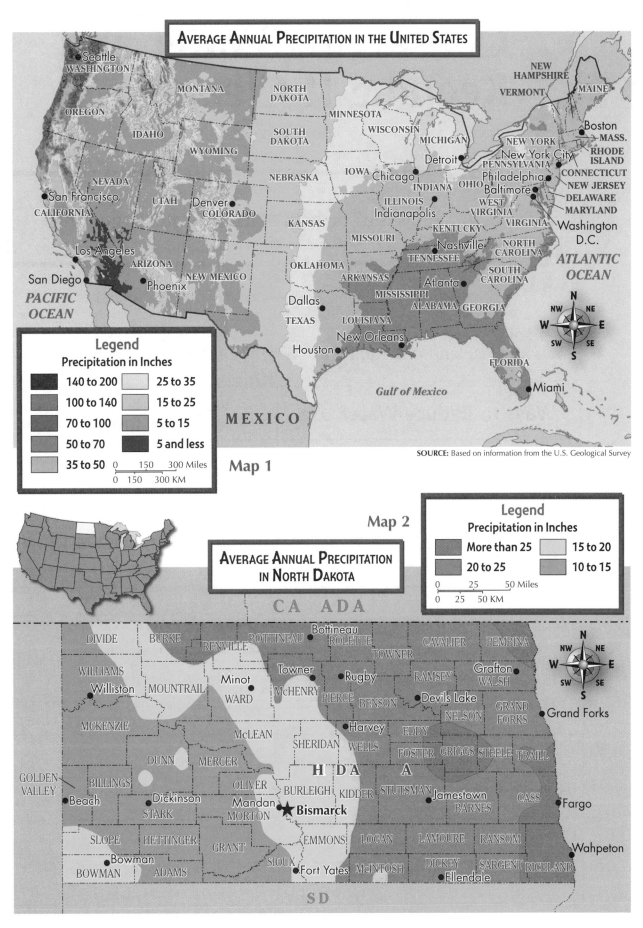

AVERAGE ANNUAL PRECIPITATION IN THE UNITED STATES

Legend
Precipitation in Inches

- 140 to 200
- 100 to 140
- 70 to 100
- 50 to 70
- 35 to 50
- 25 to 35
- 15 to 25
- 5 to 15
- 5 and less

0   150   300 Miles
0   150   300 KM

Map 1

SOURCE: Based on information from the U.S. Geological Survey

Map 2

Legend
Precipitation in Inches

- More than 25
- 20 to 25
- 15 to 20
- 10 to 15

0   25   50 Miles
0   25   50 KM

AVERAGE ANNUAL PRECIPITATION IN NORTH DAKOTA

Conserving Water and Keeping It Clean

How can you help to reduce water pollution?

1. Read the tips on Appendix page 106 about ways to reduce water use and pollution. Complete the table.

Ways to Reduce Water Use	Ways to Reduce Water Pollution

2. We all use lots of water every day. Look at Appendix page 106 to find out how much water it takes to do the things listed below.

Daily Activity	Amount of Water Used
washing the car	
using the dishwasher	
taking a shower	
running the washing machine	

3. How can you tell if your community has a water pollution problem? Ask a few adults what they know. Read local newspapers or ask your state department of natural resources. Find answers to these questions:

Do fish, frogs, ducks, and other animals live in local lakes and rivers? Are these animals healthy? _____

_____

Are the fish caught in local rivers and lakes safe to eat?

_____

4. Make a list of animals that live near your community that depend upon clean water. Where do you think these animals find drinking water? _____

_____

5. Your water could come from many sources. Your community water department may pump it from wells, from a river, or from a reservoir. Your family may pump water from your own well. Find out where your water comes from. Write what you find out in the space below.

_____

_____

6. Try this activity to better understand the water cycle. You will need a large bowl, a mug, some clear plastic wrap, and some water. Take the bowl outside and place it in a sunny spot. Fill it partly full of water and put the empty mug in the center of the bowl. Cover the bowl with plastic wrap.

Let the bowl sit in the sun for a couple of hours. The diagram on page 68 will help you understand what happens in the bowl. Write your description in the space below.

_____

_____

_____

_____

_____

San Francisco: City of Neighborhoods

San Francisco, California, sits on the tip of the San Francisco Peninsula. (A **peninsula** is a length of land that extends into a body of water.) The city overlooks San Francisco Bay to the east and the Pacific Ocean to the west.

Many large earthquakes have hit San Francisco. The most famous one happened in 1906 and destroyed much of the city. After the 1906 earthquake, San Franciscans rebuilt their city. The opening of the Golden Gate Bridge in the late 1930s improved transportation. The city experienced another period of growth in the 1940s because of its importance as a military base. In the 1960s, San Francisco became famous for a wide variety of arts. Young people from all over the world came to the city to experience the youth culture that had sprung up there. Today, the city is an important center of the computer industry.

Many neighborhoods in San Francisco are known throughout the world. A neighborhood is a smaller community inside a larger city. Some neighborhoods developed because the people who live there share the same race, culture, language, or religion.

Other neighborhoods are built around a physical feature, like one of San Francisco's famous hills. Russian Hill is famous for Lombard Street, often called "the crookedest street in the world."

There is a lot to do in San Francisco. You can ride cable cars up and down the hills of the city. You can also visit the shops and restaurants of Fisherman's Wharf or take in a Giants baseball game or 49ers football game. More than 150 parks, such as Golden Gate Park, the Presidio, and Angel Island, offer activities such as boating, sailing, hiking, or just relaxing.

The Golden Gate Bridge connects San Francisco with Marin County to the north.

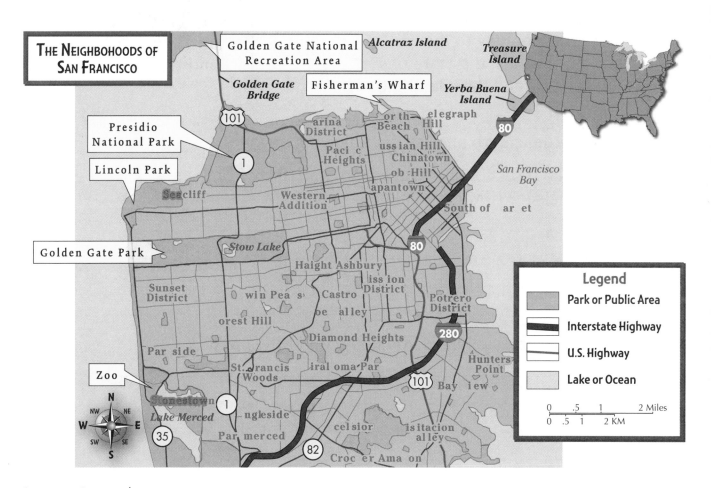

THE NEIGHBOHOODS OF SAN FRANCISCO

Golden Gate National Recreation Area

Alcatraz Island

Treasure Island

Golden Gate Bridge

Fisherman's Wharf

Yerba Buena Island

Presidio National Park

Lincoln Park

Seacliff

Golden Gate Park

Sunset District

Zoo

Stonestown

Lake Merced

Par merced

Par side

St. rancis Woods

ngleside

celsior

Croc er Ama on

arina District

Paci c Heights

Western Addition

Stow Lake

win Pea s

orest Hill

Diamond Heights

Haight Ashbury

iss ion District

Castro

be alley

iral oma Par

or th Beach

Telegraph Hill

ussian Hill

Chinatown

ob Hill

apantown

South of ar et

Potrero District

Hunters Point

Bay iew

isitacion alley

San Francisco Bay

Legend
▨	Park or Public Area
▬	Interstate Highway
▭	U.S. Highway
▨	Lake or Ocean

0 .5 1   2 Miles
0 .5 1   2 KM

N NW NE W E SW SE S

Build Your
Map Skills

Reading a State Park Map

An **island** is land that is completely surrounded by water. The map on page 77 shows Angel Island State Park, which is located in San Francisco Bay.

Between 1910 and 1940, Angel Island was a place where immigrants arriving in America were received into the country. (An **immigrant** is someone who leaves one country to live in another.) In 1963, the State of California turned the island into a park.

San Francisco is known for its cable cars.

Use the map to answer the following questions.

1. Which direction is Angel Island State Park from San Francisco? How do you know?

_____

_____

_____

_____

2. Name three activities you could do in the park.

_____

_____

_____

_____

3. A **point** is a landform that extends into a lake or ocean. It is like a peninsula but smaller. What point of land on Angel Island is furthest to the west?

_____

4. Would it be a good idea to go hiking across Point Blunt? Why or why not?

_____

_____

_____

5. A **cove** is a dish-shaped water form in a lake or ocean that extends into the land. What cove is used for a harbor on the northwest side of the island?

_____

6. What is another name for the immigration station?

_____

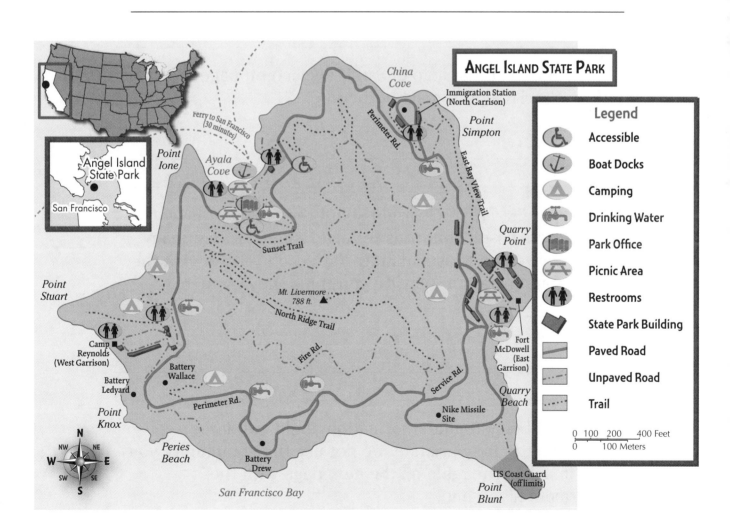

What Makes a City?

Something to Think About

What makes a community unique?

1. Look again at the material about San Francisco on pages 74–75. Describe three special things about San Francisco.

_____

_____

_____

2. Look closely at the map of San Francisco on page 75. Name three San Francisco neighborhoods.

_____

_____

_____

3. On pages 76–77, you learned about the immigrants who came from far-off countries to Angel Island. Today, many people go to Angel Island State Park each year to visit the immigration station. Why do you think they go there?

_____

_____

_____

_____

4. Use the library to find information about two large communities in your state. Do not use the community you live in. Fill in the table on the next page with the information you find.

	Community Name:	Community Name:
Population		
Geography (location, climate, nearby landforms and water forms)		
Cultural activities (museums, festivals, theaters, and so on)		
Major businesses and industries		
Fun things to do		

5. Find out if the two communities you have chosen have any special neighborhoods. If so, write their names and describe them on the lines below.

_____

_____

_____

_____

A Lobster Town in Maine

For many old towns along the coast of Maine, tourists have become more important than lobster fishing. People enjoy strolling along the piers, shopping, or just enjoying the beautiful view. But Stonington, Maine, is still a true lobster town. In fact, lobstering is more important there than ever before.

The fishing industry began in the area soon after Europeans arrived in 1755. Lobstering began about 100 years later. Shipyards, sawmills, and other factories grew in the area.

In Stonington, most of those old businesses are gone now. Almost no one fishes for cod, scallops, or shrimp anymore. They became harder to find. The government passed laws limiting the size of the fishermen's catch and how many days they could work.

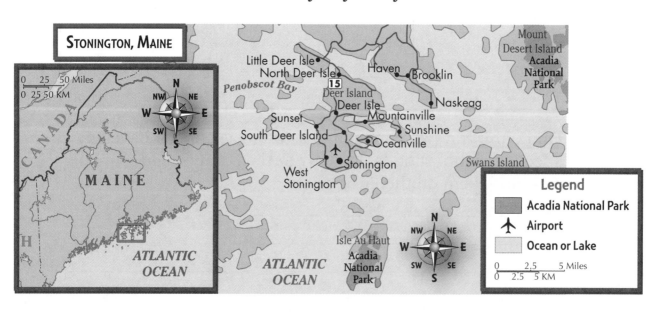

Lobstering is very important to Stonington, Maine.

But the lobstering is still good. Twenty years ago, only about 100 fishing boats sailed from Stonington Harbor. Now, there are 350. Almost all of them fish only for lobster. Today, Maine's overall lobster catch is three times larger than it was 10 or 15 years ago.

If Stonington's economy is built around lobstering, what will happen if the lobsters go away? Will Stonington become just another place to vacation, like so many other old Maine fishing towns? Further south, many lobsters are being killed by shell disease. Maine's waters are cleaner than they used to be, but it is not known if that will keep the shell disease away.

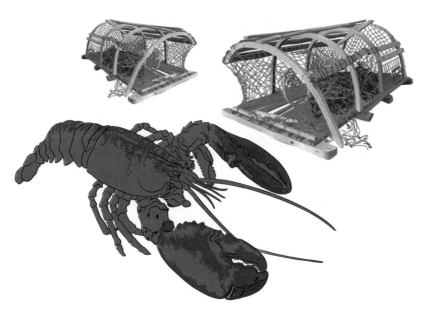

Build Your Map Skills

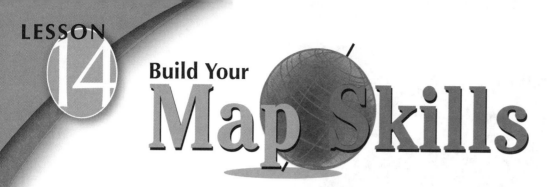

Understanding Latitude and Longitude

Fishermen and other sailors need accurate maps to find their way around the ocean. One way they do this is by using lines of latitude and longitude. These are imaginary lines that help people find their way on a journey on the water or on land.

As you have learned, the equator is an imaginary line drawn around the center of Earth. More lines are drawn parallel to the equator. These are called lines (or parallels) of **latitude.** The latitude of any place on Earth is its distance north or south of the equator, measured in degrees. The equator is 0°. The latitude of the North Pole is 90°N (this is read as "ninety degrees north"). What do you think the latitude of the South Pole is? Right—it's 90°S ("ninety degrees south"). For a comparison, the latitude of New York City is about 41°N ("41 degrees north").

The **prime meridian** is an imaginary line around Earth from the North Pole to the South Pole that runs through the city of Greenwich, England. Other lines drawn parallel to the prime meridian are called lines (or meridians) of **longitude.** Like latitude, longitude is measured in degrees. The longitude of New York City is 74°W ("seventy-four degrees west").

The equator divides Earth into the northern and southern hemispheres. The prime meridian divides Earth into the western and eastern hemispheres. **Hemisphere** means "half of a globe."

Use the map of the globe and the information above to answer the questions. You may also refer to Lesson 1, if necessary, for information on the continents and oceans.

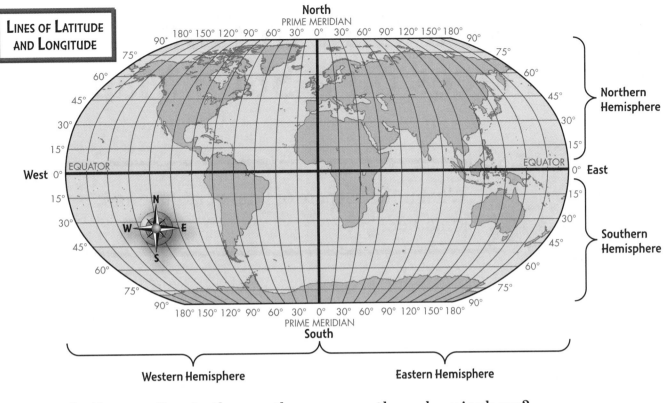

LINES OF LATITUDE AND LONGITUDE

North
PRIME MERIDIAN

Northern Hemisphere

EQUATOR

West 0°   0° East

Southern Hemisphere

PRIME MERIDIAN
South

Western Hemisphere   Eastern Hemisphere

1. Do you live in the northern or southern hemisphere?

_____

2. Do you live in the eastern or western hemisphere?

_____

3. Name one continent that is completely in the southern hemisphere.

_____

4. The continent of Africa is within what hemispheres?

_____

_____

_____

5. Find 15°S latitude. Now find 60°W longitude. Follow the two lines until they meet. On what continent do the two lines meet?

_____

6. Find 0° latitude. Now find 90°E longitude. On what ocean do these two lines meet?

_____

Use a Grid to Find Places on a State Map

Something to Think About

What is the purpose of lines of latitude and longitude?

The map shows the major degrees of latitude and longitude that cross the state of Maine. These lines of latitude and longitude create a grid across the state. The place where a line of latitude and a line of longitude meet is called a **coordinate.**

To better understand this, put a ruler across the map at 47°N latitude and draw a line with a pencil across the state. Now put the ruler across the map at 68°W longitude and draw another line across the state. The place where the two lines meet is the *coordinate* named 47°N latitude, 68°W longitude.

In this activity, you will use lines of latitude and longitude to find places on a state map.

1. Flagstaff Lake is just north of what latitude?

   _____

2. What city is closest to 47°N latitude and 68°W longitude?

   _____

3. What lakes are between 69°W longitude and 70°W longitude?

   _____

4. What city is closest to 45°N latitude and 69°W longitude?

   _____

5. Penobscot Bay is at about what grid coordinate?

   _____

6. What city is just west of 44°N latitude and 70°W longitude?

_____

7. Find where 47°N latitude and 67°W longitude meet. Use directions to describe this location.

_____

_____

8. What state appears west of about 71°W longitude?

_____

9. Which general direction would you travel from the city of Portland to the coordinate 45°N latitude, 68°W longitude?

_____

10. What river extends in a north/south direction between 69°W and 70°W longitude?

_____

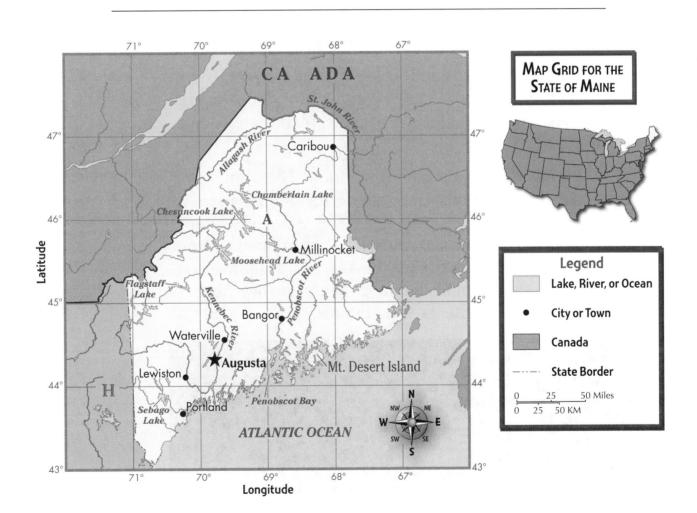

Beautiful Parks

Many communities have parks. Some parks are more like playgrounds. But parks can also help educate people about nature. Parks teach people about the kinds of plants and animals that live in an area. The place where an animal or plant lives is called its **habitat.**

There are many different types of habitats. For example, young forests are perfect habitats for deer and small animals who find plenty of plants to eat and hiding places there. Woodpeckers can be found in older forests, because they have many dead trees full of insects. Frogs and salamanders are often found in ponds and creeks.

All living things need the same things: a place to live, water, and food. Plants use sunlight and water to make their own food. Because of this, plants are called **producers.**

Animals can't make their own food. They must eat plants or other animals. Because of this, animals are called **consumers.** Some consumers, like grasshoppers, mice, rabbits, beaver, and moose, eat only plants. Other consumers, like frogs, snakes, hawks, and spiders, mostly eat other animals. Some consumers, like bears or turtles, eat both plants and animals.

Parks can help to educate people about nature.

Then, there are the **decomposers.** Decomposers, like insects, eat decaying things, like dead animals and plants. They also help release chemicals into the soil for plants to use. Fungi, like mushrooms, and bacteria are also decomposers.

A **food chain** shows how each living thing gets its food. Look at the food chain shown in Diagram 1. Can you name the producers? Can you name the consumers and decomposers?

An **organism** is a living thing. Every organism in a food chain depends on other organisms for survival. What do you think would happen to the food chain in Diagram 1 if the plants did not grow? Parks can help us all learn about natural processes like the food chain.

Every habitat has producers, consumers, and decomposers.

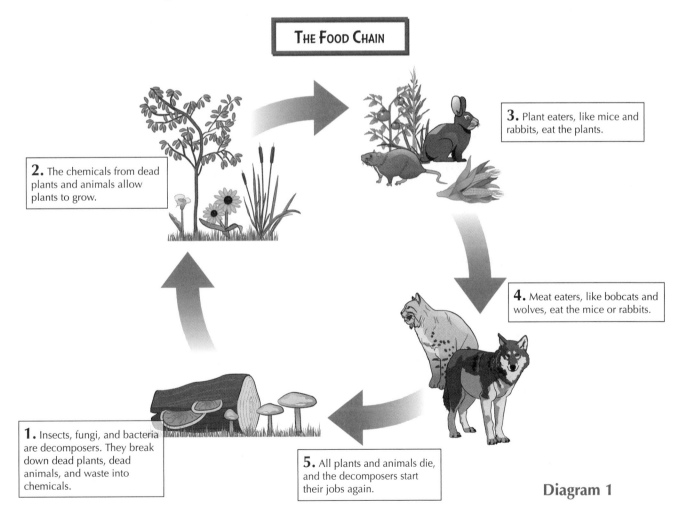

THE FOOD CHAIN

2. The chemicals from dead plants and animals allow plants to grow.

3. Plant eaters, like mice and rabbits, eat the plants.

4. Meat eaters, like bobcats and wolves, eat the mice or rabbits.

1. Insects, fungi, and bacteria are decomposers. They break down dead plants, dead animals, and waste into chemicals.

5. All plants and animals die, and the decomposers start their jobs again.

Diagram 1

Build Your Map Skills

Using a City Park Map

As you have learned, a city park can teach us much about the natural world. Eden Park in Cincinnati, Ohio, is considered one of the most beautiful city parks in America. The park's 186 acres are visited by joggers, hikers, and families who want to get away from the noise of the city.

In this activity, you will lead a nature group on a tour exploring Eden Park. Before your group meets, make sure you know how to read the park map. Match these symbols in the map legend with their descriptions below.

A. 〜	C. ▨
B. 🛝	D. 👓

_____B_____ **1.** You feel like playing on the swings for a while. Which map symbol shows you where they are located?

_____ **2.** Which map symbol will help you find the park's prairie land?

_____ **3.** You would like to visit a spot in the park that has a great view. Which map symbol will you look for?

_____ **4.** Which map symbol can help you avoid steep areas so you don't fall down a hill?

5. A member of the group wants to know how to get to the parking lot near Twin Lakes. She will be entering the park on Fulton Avenue. Using landmarks and the compass rose, write directions for her. _____

_____

_____

_____

6. Describe to the nature group how you can get to the prairie area from the trailhead north of Mirror Lake. _____

_____

_____

_____

_____

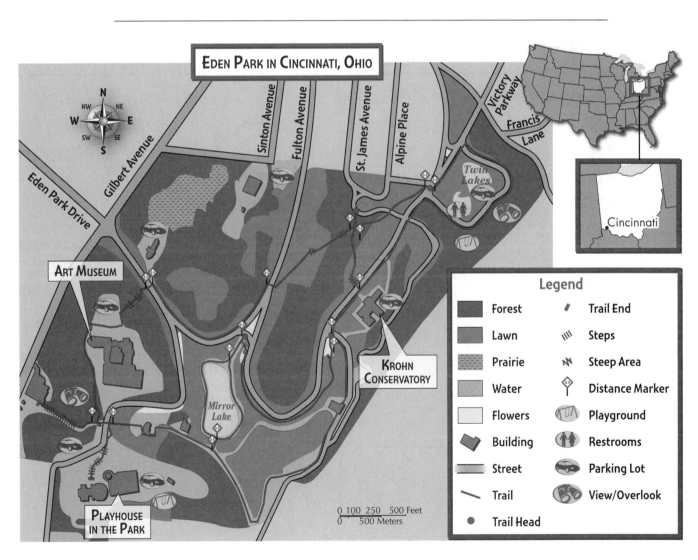

EDEN PARK IN CINCINNATI, OHIO

Gilbert Avenue

Eden Park Drive

Sinton Avenue

Fulton Avenue

St. James Avenue

Alpine Place

Victory Parkway

Francis Lane

Twin Lakes

Cincinnati

ART MUSEUM

KROHN CONSERVATORY

Mirror Lake

PLAYHOUSE IN THE PARK

0 100 250   500 Feet
0   500 Meters

Legend

Forest

Lawn

Prairie

Water

Flowers

Building

Street

Trail

● Trail Head

Trail End

Steps

Steep Area

Distance Marker

Playground

Restrooms

Parking Lot

View/Overlook

Learn about the Food Chain

Something **to** **Think** About

How are people affected by the food chain?

1. Write whether each organism below is a producer, a consumer, or a decomposer.

Organisms	Role in Food Chain

Organisms	Role in Food Chain

2. Look again at the stages of the food chain in the diagram on page 87. On a separate piece of paper, draw a food chain with at least four organisms. Use organisms that live in habitats in or near your community. Label each member of the food chain as a producer, a consumer, or a decomposer.

3. Think about ways that human beings affect the land and water where they live. Describe one way that the things human beings do might affect each of the organisms in the food chain shown below.

Producer

Trees

_____
_____

Consumer

Duck

_____
_____

Consumer (meat eater)

Bat

_____
_____

4. How do you think your place in a food chain could be affected by water pollution that kills fish? If you need to, ask some adults for their thoughts or read about pollution in newspapers or magazines. _____

_____

_____

_____

_____

Appendix

Strait of Juan de Fuca

Cape Flattery
Puget Sound
Seattle
Tacoma
Olympia ★

Mt. Rainier
14,410 ft.
(4,392 m.)

COLUMBIA
PLATEAU

WASHINGTON

Portland

Salem ★

Mt. Hood
11,235 ft.
(3,424 m.)

OREGON

Boise ★

IDAHO

Mt. Shasta
14,162 ft.
(4,316 m.)

Borah Peak
12,662 ft.
(3,859 m.)

Snake R.

Grand
Teton Peak
13,770 ft.
(4,197 m.)

ROCKY

BITTERROOT RANGE

Helena ★

Missouri R.

Fort Peck
Lake

Yellowstone R.

MONTANA

Lake Sakakawea

NORTH DAKO

★ Bismarck

SOUTH DAKO

Lake Oah

★ Pierre

BIGHORN MTNS.

WYOMING

BLACK
HILLS

GREAT

Cape
Mendocino

COAST RANGES

CASCADE RANGE

Columbia R.

GREAT
BASIN

GREAT
SALT LAKE
DESERT

Salt Lake City ★

Great
Salt
Lake

WASATCH RANGE

MOUNTAINS

Continental Divide

North Platte R.

Platte R.

NEBRASKA

Cheyenne ★

PLAINS

K

Sacramento ★

San Francisco
Oakland

San Jose ●

NEVADA

Carson City ★

Mt. Elbert
14,433 ft.
(4,399 m.)

Green R.

Denver ★
Pikes Peak
14,110 ft.
(4,301 m.)

South Platte R.

Fresno ●

Mt. Whitney
14,496 ft.
(4,418 m.)

SIERRA NEVADA

Death Valley
-282 ft.
(-89 m.)

Las Vegas ●

UTAH

Lake
Mead

Lake
Powell

COLORADO

COLORADO
PLATEAU

PAINTED
DESERT

Arkansas R.

CALIFORNIA

Point Conception

MOJAVE
DESERT

Grand Canyon

Colorado R.

ARIZONA

SANGRE DE
CRISTO MTNS.

Santa Fe ★

OKL

Oklahoma Cit

Los Angeles ●
Long Beach ●

San Bernardino ●

Riverside ●

San Diego ●

Glendale ●
Phoenix ●
Mesa ●

Divide

Tucson ●

Continental

NEW MEXICO

LLANNO
ESTACADO

Fort Wor

*Pacific
Ocean*

Gulf of
California

El Paso ●

Rio Grande

Mexico

EDWARDS
PLATEAU

TEXA

Austin ★

San Antonio ●

Alaska inset

174° 178° 174° 170° 166° 162° 158° 154° 150° 146° 142° 138° 134° 130°

70°

Chukchi Sea

Point Barrow

Beaufort Sea

Russia

BROOKS RANGE

Mt. McKinley
20,320 ft.
(6,194 m.)

Yukon R.

SEWARD
PEN.

Canada

Bering Strait

ALASKA

ALASKA RANGE

Tanana R.

Bering Sea

Iliamna Lake

Gulf of Alaska

58°

Bristol Bay

Juneau

0   200 Miles

0   200 KM

ALASKA PEN.

Shelikof Strait

54°

ALEUTIAN ISLANDS

Pacific Ocean

174° 178° 174° 170° 166° 162° 158° 154° 150° 146° 142° 138° 134° 130°

Hawaii inset

160° 159° 158° 157° 156° 155°

22°

Kauai
Channel

HAWAII

Honolulu ●

21°

*Pacific
Ocean*

Alenuihaha Channel

0   100 Miles

0   100 KM

Mauna Kea
13,796 ft.
(4,205 m.)

20°

19°

160° 159° 158° 157° 156° 155°

120°   115°   110°   100°

Canada

Lake of
the Woods

MINNESOTA

Lake Superior

MICHIGAN

WISCONSIN

Minneapolis ★
Saint Paul ★

Lake Michigan

Lake Huron

Milwaukee ●
Madison ★

Grand Rapids ●
Lansing ★
Detroit ●

IOWA

ILLINOIS

Chicago ●
Hammond ● Gary ●

OHIO

Toledo ●

CENTRAL LOWLAND

es Moines ★

Springfield ★

Indianapolis ★

INDIANA

Dayton ●

Akron ●
Canton ●

Cleveland ●
Youngstown ●

Kansas
City ●

Saint
Louis ●

Columbus ★

Cincinnati ●

Jefferson City ★

MISSOURI

Louisville ●

KENTUCKY

Frankfort ★

OZARK
PLATEAU

OZARK PLATEAU

Cumberland R.

WEST
VIRGINIA

Charleston ★

A

ARKANSAS

TENNESSEE

Nashville ★

Knoxville ●

Little Rock ★

Memphis ●

Tennessee R.

CUMBERLAND

APPALACHIAN MOUNTAINS

Mt. Mitchell
6,684 ft.
(2,037 m.)

Birmingham ●

Atlanta ●

Columbia ★

SOUTH
CAROLINA

LOUISIANA

Jackson ★

ALABAMA

Montgomery ★

GEORGIA

MISSISSIPPI

Chattahoochee R.

COASTAL PLAIN

Jacksonville ●

Baton Rouge ★

Lake
Pontchartrain

Tallahassee ★

New Orleans ●

FLORIDA

Orlando ●

Tampa ●

Gulf of
Mexico

Saint Petersburg ●

Lake
Okeechobee

Cape Canaveral

Miami ●

Cape Sable

Straits of Florida

The
Bahamas

Lake
Champlain

St Lawrence R.

MAINE

Mt. Washington
6,288 ft.
(1,905 m.)

Augusta ★

ADIRONDACK MTNS.

VT.

Montpelier ★

NH.

Concord ★

Lake
Ontario

Rochester ●

Syracuse ●

Albany ★

Boston ●

MASS.

Niagara Falls ●

Buffalo ●

NEW
YORK

Hartford ★

Providence ★

RHODE
ISLAND

Susquehanna
River

New Haven ●

CONNECTICUT

Lake Erie

Cleveland ●

PENNSYLVANIA

Newark ●

New York ●

Harrisburg ★

Philadelphia ●

NEW JERSEY

Pittsburgh ●

Trenton ★

Camden ●

Baltimore ●

Dover ★

Delaware Bay

DELAWARE

Washington D.C. ⊛

Annapolis ★

MARYLAND

Ohio R.

Richmond ★

Chesapeake Bay

Newport News ●

VIRGINIA

Norfolk ●

Roanoke R.

Winston-Salem ●

Raleigh ★

Cape Hatteras

Atlantic
Ocean

NORTH CAROLINA

Wabash R.

Mississippi R.

Missouri R.

Alabama R.

Legend

⊛	National Capital
★	State Capital
●	Major City
—	International boundary
–·–	State boundary

N
NW NE
W E
SW SE
S

| 0 | 125 | 250 | 500 Miles |
| 0 | 125 | 250 | 500 KM |

NORTH AMERICA

ICELAND

RUSSIA

KALAALLIT NUNAAT (GREENLAND) (DENMARK)

CANADA

North Pole

Arctic Ocean

Greenland Sea

Denmark Strait

Cape Farewell

Labrador Sea

Newfoundland

Gulf of St. Lawrence Nova

LABRADOR

Smallwood Res.

Davis Strait

Cape Howe

Ungava Bay

UNGAVA PEN.

Nares Strait

Baffin Bay

Baffin Island

Hudson Strait

Ellesmere Island

MELVILLE PEN.

Hudson Bay

Queen Elizabeth Islands

Prince of Wales Island

BOOTHIA PEN.

Churchill

Lake Nipigon

Victoria Island

CANADIAN SHIELD

Lake Winnipeg

Winnipeg

Banks Island

Great Bear Lake

Lake Athabasca

Nelson R.

Lake Manitoba

Regina

Beaufort Sea

Great Slave Lake

Churchill R.

North Saskatchewan R.

South Saskatchewan R.

Calgary

Point Barrow

Mackenzie R.

Peace R.

Athabasca R.

Edmonton

Spokane

MACKENZIE MOUNTAINS

BROOKS RANGE

Fairbanks

Whitehorse

ROCKY MOUNTAINS

Vancouver

SEWARD PEN.

Bering Strait

Chukchi Sea

Mt. Logan 19,551 ft. (5,959 m.)

Juneau

COAST MOUNTAINS

Victoria

Seattle

ALASKA RANGE

Yukon R.

Fraser R.

Bering Sea

Saint Lawrence Island

Mt. McKinley 20,320 ft. (6,194 m.)

Anchorage

Gulf of Alaska

Alexander Archipelago

Queen Charlotte Islands

Vancouver Island

Portland

0°

15°W

75°W

North Pole

75°N

180°W

165°W

150°W

45°N

60°N

60°N

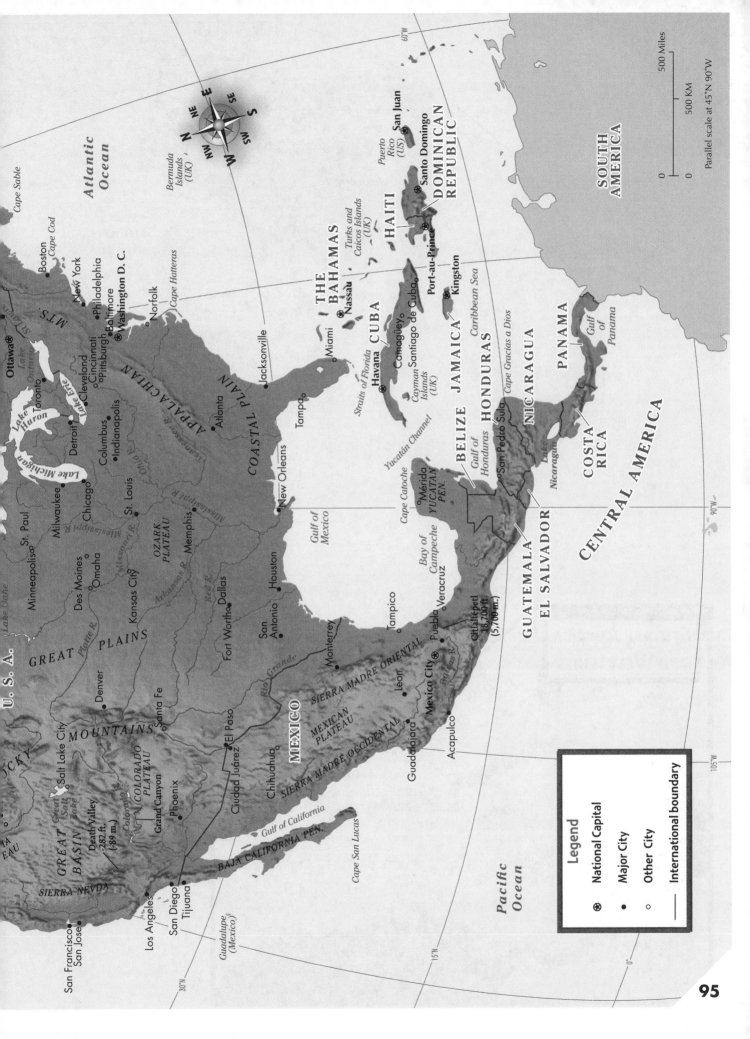

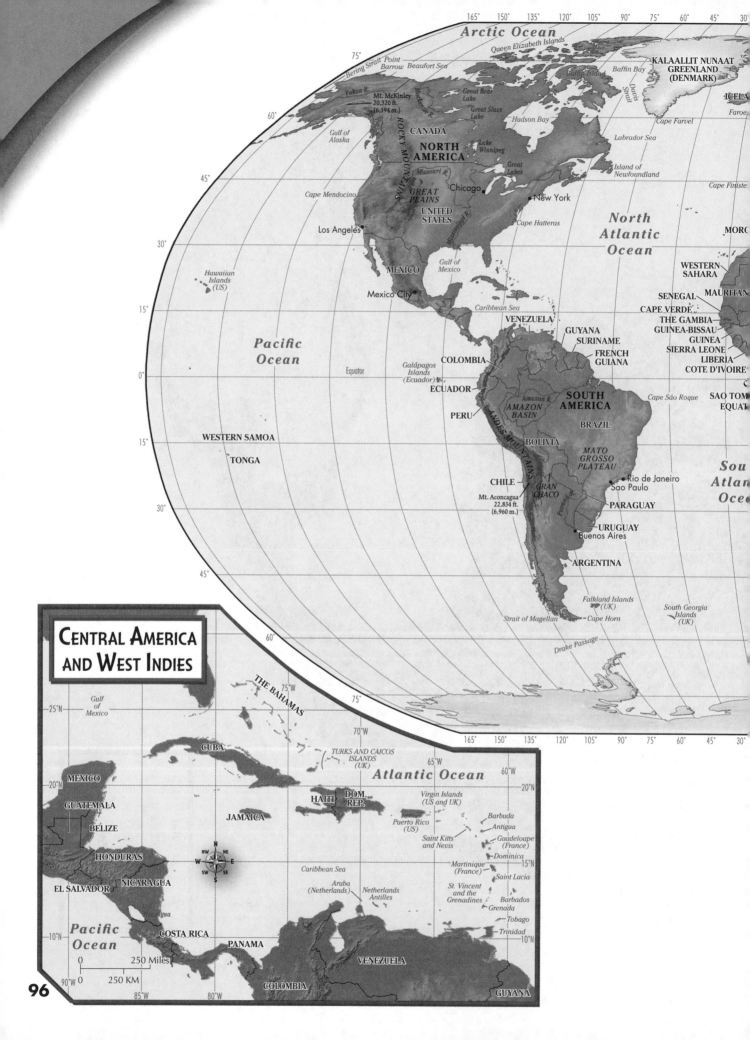

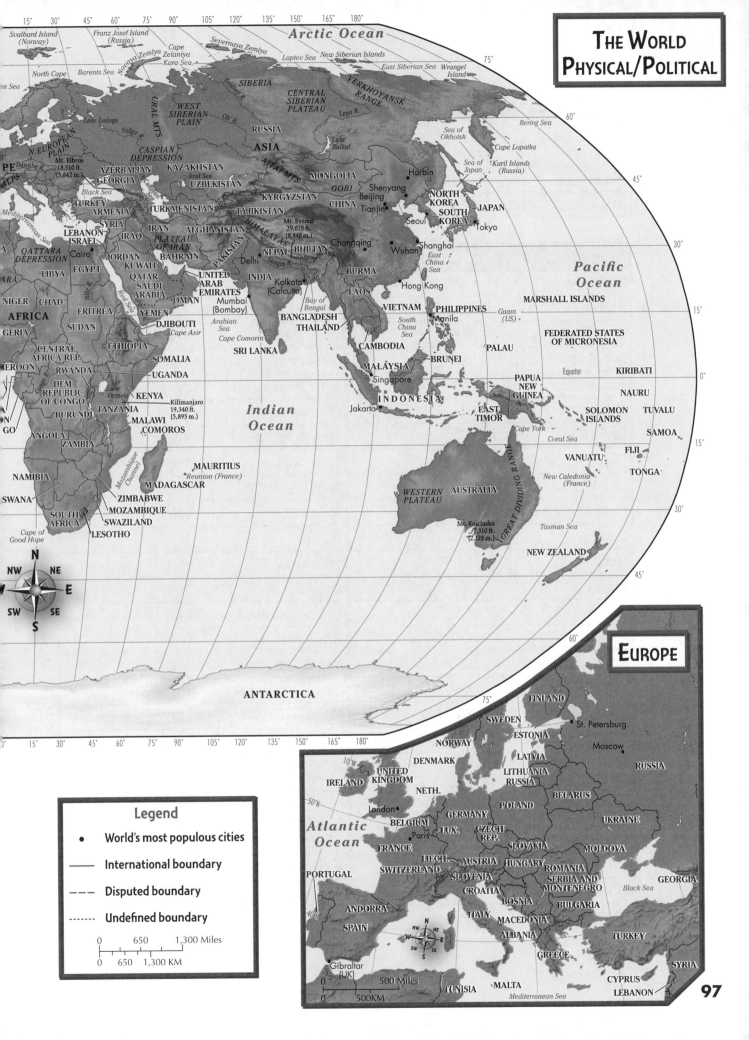

Arctic Ocean

Svalbard Island (Norway)
Franz Josef Island (Russia)
Cape Zelaniya
Kara Sea
Severnaya Zemlya
Laptev Sea
New Siberian Islands
East Siberian Sea
Wrangel Island

North Cape
Barents Sea
Novaya Zemlya
SIBERIA
CENTRAL SIBERIAN PLATEAU
VERKHOYANSK RANGE
Bering Sea

en Sea
URAL MTS.
WEST SIBERIAN PLAIN
RUSSIA
ASIA
Lena R.
Sea of Okhotsk
Cape Lopatka

N. EUROPEAN PLAIN
Volga R.
CASPIAN DEPRESSION
Lake Ladoga
Ob' R.
Yenisey R.
Lake Baikal
ALTAI MTS.
MONGOLIA
Harbin
Sea of Japan
Kuril Islands (Russia)

PE
ALPS
Mt. Elbrus 18,510 ft. (5,642 m.)
AZERBAIJAN
GEORGIA
KAZAKHSTAN
Aral Sea
UZBEKISTAN
KYRGYZSTAN
GOBI
Shenyang
Beijing
Tianjin
NORTH KOREA
SOUTH KOREA
JAPAN
Danube R.
Black Sea
TURKEY
ARMENIA
SYRIA
TURKMENISTAN
TAJIKISTAN
CHINA
Seoul
Tokyo
Mediterranean Sea
LEBANON
ISRAEL
IRAN
IRAQ
PLATEAU OF IRAN
AFGHANISTAN
HIMALAYAS
Mt. Everest 29,028 ft. (8,848 m.)
NEPAL
BHUTAN
Chongqing
Wuhan
Shanghai
A
QATTARA DEPRESSION
JORDAN
KUWAIT
BAHRAIN
Cairo
EGYPT
QATAR
SAUDI ARABIA
UNITED ARAB EMIRATES
Delhi
Ganges R.
INDIA
Kolkata (Calcutta)
BURMA
East China Sea
Hong Kong
Pacific Ocean

ARA
LIBYA
Red Sea
Nile R.
OMAN
Mumbai (Bombay)
Bay of Bengal
LAOS
VIETNAM
PHILIPPINES
MARSHALL ISLANDS

NIGER
CHAD
ERITREA
YEMEN
DJIBOUTI
SUDAN
Arabian Sea
Cape Asir
Cape Comorin
BANGLADESH
THAILAND
South China Sea
Manila
Guam (US)
FEDERATED STATES OF MICRONESIA

AFRICA
GERIA
CENTRAL AFRICA REP.
EROON
ETHIOPIA
SOMALIA
UGANDA
SRI LANKA
CAMBODIA
PALAU
KIRIBATI

RWANDA
DEM. REPUBLIC OF CONGO
Lake Victoria
KENYA
Kilimanjaro 19,340 ft. (5,895 m.)
MALAYSIA
Singapore
Equator
NAURU

N
GO
BURUNDI
TANZANIA
MALAWI
COMOROS
INDONESIA
Jakarta
PAPUA NEW GUINEA
EAST TIMOR
SOLOMON ISLANDS
TUVALU

ANGOLA
ZAMBIA
Mozambique Channel
Indian Ocean
Cape York
Coral Sea
New Caledonia (France)
SAMOA

NAMIBIA
MAURITIUS
Reunion (France)
MADAGASCAR
VANUATU
FIJI

SWANA
ZIMBABWE
MOZAMBIQUE
SWAZILAND
WESTERN PLATEAU
AUSTRALIA
GREAT DIVIDING RANGE
TONGA

SOUTH AFRICA
LESOTHO
Cape of Good Hope
Mt. Kosciusko 7,310 ft. (2,228 m.)
Tasman Sea

NEW ZEALAND

**N
NW NE
W E
SW SE
S**

ANTARCTICA

Legend

• World's most populous cities

⎯⎯ International boundary

– – – Disputed boundary

······· Undefined boundary

0   650   1,300 Miles
0   650   1,300 KM

FINLAND
SWEDEN
St. Petersburg
Moscow
NORWAY
ESTONIA
LATVIA
LITHUANIA
RUSSIA
RUSSIA
DENMARK
UNITED KINGDOM
IRELAND
NETH.
POLAND
BELARUS
UKRAINE
London
GERMANY
Atlantic Ocean
BELGIUM
Paris
LUX.
CZECH REP.
SLOVAKIA
MOLDOVA
FRANCE
LIECH.
AUSTRIA
HUNGARY
ROMANIA
GEORGIA
SWITZERLAND
SLOVENIA
SERBIA AND MONTENEGRO
Black Sea
PORTUGAL
CROATIA
BOSNIA
BULGARIA
ANDORRA
ITALY
MACEDONIA
SPAIN
ALBANIA
TURKEY
Gibraltar (UK)
GREECE
CYPRUS
SYRIA
TUNISIA
MALTA
Mediterranean Sea
LEBANON

**N
NW NE
W E
SW SE
S**

0   500 Miles
0   500KM

97

The Seven Continents	
Africa	Europe
Antarctica	North America
Asia	South America
Australia	

Oceans of the World
Arctic
Atlantic
Indian
Pacific

State Names and Abbreviations			
State Name	**Abbreviation**	**State Name**	**Abbreviation**
Alabama	AL	Montana	MT
Alaska	AK	Nebraska	NE
Arizona	AZ	Nevada	NV
Arkansas	AR	New Hampshire	NH
California	CA	New Jersey	NJ
Colorado	CO	New Mexico	NM
Connecticut	CT	New York	NY
Delaware	DE	North Carolina	NC
Florida	FL	North Dakota	ND
Georgia	GA	Ohio	OH
Hawaii	HI	Oklahoma	OK
Idaho	ID	Oregon	OR
Illinois	IL	Pennsylvania	PA
Indiana	IN	Rhode Island	RI
Iowa	IA	South Carolina	SC
Kansas	KS	South Dakota	SD
Kentucky	KY	Tennessee	TN
Louisiana	LA	Texas	TX
Maine	ME	Utah	UT
Maryland	MD	Vermont	VT
Massachusetts	MA	Virginia	VA
Michigan	MI	Washington	WA
Minnesota	MN	West Virginia	WV
Mississippi	MS	Wisconsin	WI
Missouri	MO	Wyoming	WY

Animals from Around the World

Name of Animal	Native Continent	Interesting Fact
Bengal tiger	Asia	Bengal tigers hunt mostly at night. By day, they hide in the tall grasses where they live.
Giant panda	Asia	The panda's main food is bamboo. A panda can eat over 80 pounds of bamboo shoots in a day. They like to eat honey, too.
Giraffe	Africa	Giraffes don't need much sleep. They only sleep 20 minutes to 2 hours every day.
Gorilla	Africa	Gorillas live in forests in groups of up to 30. Each group is led by an adult male who is called a *silverback*. Gorillas do not drink water—they get their water from the plants they eat.
Kangaroo	Australia	Baby kangaroos are called *joeys*. A mother kangaroo carries a joey in a special pouch.
Koala	Australia	Koalas live almost entirely on eucalyptus leaves. These leaves are poison to many other animals. Koalas almost never come out of the trees where they live.
Ostrich	Africa	Ostriches are considered the largest living species of bird. They do not fly, but they can run up to 45 miles per hour.
Penguin	Antarctica	There are 17 species of penguins, and all of them live in the Southern Hemisphere. Emperor Penguins weigh up to 75 pounds. Little Blue Penguins weigh only about 2 pounds.
Platypus	Australia	The platypus is an odd-looking animal. When it was first described to scientists in Europe, some did not believe that this unusual creature existed.
Zebra	Africa	Some scientists think that the zebra's stripes confuse bloodsucking flies that live nearby.

Types of Maps

Different types of maps are made to show different things. Here are some of the most common types of maps.

- **Climate maps** show information about what the weather is usually like at a specific place on Earth. These maps use different colors to show the different climate areas.

- **Economic** or **resource maps** tell us what kinds of natural resources (like trees) an area has or what kind of work is done there. Mapmakers use symbols to show the different resources and work. For example, a corn symbol on a map of Nebraska tells you that corn is grown there. A car symbol on a map of Michigan tells you that cars are built there.

- **Physical maps** show Earth's different landforms and water forms. Water is usually shown in blue. Different colors may be used to show differences in land elevation (the height of the land).

- **Political maps** show state and national boundaries and important cities. Capital cities are usually marked with a star. The government meets in a capital city to govern the state or the country.

- **Road maps** are a commonly used map. They show major highways, important smaller roads, and cities and towns. They also usually show the location of airports, railroad tracks, and parks. People use road maps to find their way on a trip. The scale on a road map allows a traveler to estimate the driving distance from one place to another.

- **Topographic maps** have lines that show the shape and elevation of an area. Steep areas are shown with lines that are close together. Flat areas have lines that are farther apart. These types of maps are often used by hikers.

Types of Communities

Urban communities, like the cities of Chicago, New York, and San Francisco, are very busy places. They are densely populated, particularly in the daytime, with people who come to work there. Except for parks, they have very little open land. Urban communities often have more apartment buildings than houses. They also have many tall office buildings and stores. These communities have many different types of transportation including cars, subways, and buses.

Suburban communities, also called *suburbs,* are usually located near urban communities. These are usually smaller towns where people live in homes or apartment buildings. Many people live in the suburbs and travel to the nearby city to work. For this reason, suburban communities are often called *bedroom communities.* There are stores in these communities to meet the needs of the residents, but usually no large skyscrapers.

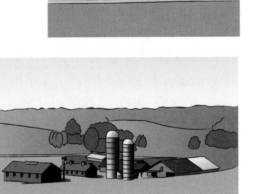

Rural communities usually have much more open land than urban or suburban communities. The homes in rural communities are often separated by woodlands and meadows. People living in rural communities often make their living through agriculture on farms or ranches.

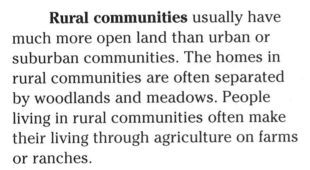

Population of Major Wyoming Communities

Community Name	Population	Community Name	Population
Casper	49,644	Jackson	8,647
Cheyenne	53,011	Laramie	27,204
Cody	8,835	Rawlins	8,538
Gillette	19,646	Rock Springs	18,708
Green River	11,808	Sheridan	15,804

SOURCE: U.S. Census Bureau, Census 2000

Focus on Arkansas

Nickname: The Natural State

Largest industries: agriculture, food processing, tourism

Major products: poultry and eggs, soybeans, sorghum, cattle, cotton, rice, hogs, milk, electric equipment, metal products, machinery, and paper products

Geography: Arkansas is a beautiful land of lush forests, mountains and valleys, and fertile plains. Northwest Arkansas is part of the Ozark Plateau and includes the Boston Mountains. The Ouachita Mountains are located in the southwest part of the state. The area of southern and eastern Arkansas is called the *lowlands*.

Facts about Arkansas:

- Mount Magazine is the state's highest point at 2,753 feet above sea level.
- The average temperature in July is 81.4 degrees. In January, it is 39.5 degrees.
- Arkansas has many official state symbols. The mockingbird is the state bird. The loblolly pine is the state tree. The apple blossom is the state flower.

- The state has six national parks, millions of acres of national forests, and 50 state parks. The Ozark National Forest covers more than one million acres.
- Ouachita National Forest is the oldest national forest in the South.
- The community of Mountain View is called the Folk Capital of America. The little town preserves and displays the pioneer way of life. Visitors pour into the Ozark Folk Center State Park from March through October.
- Arkansas contains over 600,000 acres of lakes and 9,700 miles of streams and rivers.
- There are 47 hot springs that flow from the southwestern slope of Hot Springs Mountain. They have an average temperature of 143°F.

Population of Major Arkansas Communities	
City	**Population**
Little Rock (state capital)	183,133
Fort Smith	80,268
North Little Rock	60,433
Fayetteville	58,047
Jonesboro	55,515

SOURCE: U.S. Census Bureau, Census 2000

Focus on Maine

Nickname: The Pine Tree State

Largest industries: fishing, tourism, lumber and wood products, shipbuilding

Major products: seafood, poultry and eggs, dairy products, blueberries, potatoes, maple sugar, bottled water, paper, lumber, wood products, and ships

Geography: Maine's coastal lowlands start at the Atlantic Ocean and spread from 10 to 40 miles inland. The eastern New England uplands are northwest of the coastal lowlands. This area rises to about 2,000 feet in the west and includes the Aroostook Plateau. The White Mountain region covers northwestern Maine. Mount Katahdin, Maine's highest point, is found here.

Facts about Maine:

- Maine contains 542,629 acres of state and national parks. The White Mountain National Forest covers nearly 800,000 acres.
- The White Mountains have 10 mountains over 4,000 feet high and 97 mountains over 3,000 feet high.
- The average temperature in July is 67°F. In January, it is 15°F.

- The state tree is the white pine. The state bird is the chickadee. The moose is Maine's state animal.
- Maine is farther northeast than any other state. Eastport, Maine, is further east than any other town in the United States. It is thought to be the first place in the United States to receive the rays of the morning sun.
- Approximately 40 millions pounds (nearly 90 percent) of the nation's lobster supply is caught off the coast of Maine.
- Maine produces 99 percent of all the blueberries in the country.
- Acadia National Park is the second most visited national park in the United States.

Population of Major Communities in Maine	
City	**Population**
Portland	64,249
Lewiston	35,690
Bangor	31,473
South Portland	23,324
Auburn	23,203

SOURCE: U.S. Census Bureau, Census 2000

Major U.S. Rivers

River Name	It Flows Into the	River Length
1. Missouri	Mississippi River	2,540 miles
2. Mississippi	Gulf of Mexico	2,340 miles
3. Yukon	Bering Sea	1,980 miles
4. Rio Grande	Gulf of Mexico	1,900 miles
5. St. Lawrence	Gulf of St. Lawrence	1,900 miles
6. Arkansas	Mississippi River	1,460 miles
7. Colorado	Gulf of California	1,450 miles
8. Red	Mississippi River	1,290 miles
9. Brazos	Gulf of Mexico	1,280 miles
10. Columbia	Pacific Ocean	1,240 miles
11. Snake	Columbia River	1,040 miles
12. Platte	Missouri River	990 miles
13. Ohio	Mississippi River	981 miles
14. Pecos	Gulf of Mexico	926 miles
15. Canadian	Arkansas River	906 miles
16. Tennessee	Ohio River	886 miles
17. Colorado (Texas)	Matagorda Bay	862 miles
18. North Canadian	Canadian River	800 miles
19. Mobile	Gulf of Mexico	774 miles
20. Kansas	Missouri River	743 miles
21. Kuskokwim	Bering Sea	724 miles
22. Green	Colorado River	730 miles
23. James	Missouri River	710 miles
24. Yellowstone	Missouri River	692 miles
25. Tanana	Yukon River	659 miles
26. Gila	Colorado River	630 miles
27. Milk	Missouri River	625 miles
28. Quachita	Red River	605 miles

SOURCE: U.S. Geological Survey

Selected Port Cities and Reservoirs of the Tennessee River

Paducah
Population: 25,565
- Established by William Clark in 1827
- Named after Padouca Indians

Places of Interest
- River Heritage Museum
- Paducah Railroad Museum

Nearby Parks
- Kentucky Dam Village State Resort Park
- Metropolis Lake State Nature Preserve

Chattanooga
Population: 155,554
- Established by John Ross in 1816
- Named after an Indian name for nearby Lookout Mountain.

Places of Interest
- African American Museum
- Chattanooga Regional History Museum
- Gordon Lee Mansion

Nearby Parks
- Chickamauga and Chattanooga National Military Park
- Harrison Bay State Park
- Lookout Mountain/Ruby Falls

Decatur
Population: 54,528
- Area founded as Rhodes Ferry in 1810s

Size in acres: 10,370
- Named after Commodore Stephen Decatur, an American naval hero of the War of 1812

Places of Interest
- Watts Bar Lake
- Old State Bank
- Cook's Natural Science Museum

Nearby Parks
- Rhodes Ferry Park
- Point Mallard Park
- Wheeler National Wildlife Refuge

Nickajack Lake
Shoreline: 215 miles
Size in acres: 10,370
Year dam completed: 1967

Watts Bar Lake
Shoreline: 783 miles
Size in acres: 39,000
Year dam completed: 1942

Pickwick Lake
Shoreline: 496 miles
Size in acres: 43,100
Year dam completed: 1938

Kentucky Lake
Shoreline: 2,380 miles
Size in acres: 160,000
Year dam completed: 1944

Improve Your Water Knowledge

How Much Water Does It Take To . . . ?

- Take a shower or bath? *15 to 26 gallons*
- Use the dishwasher? *7 to 16 gallons*
- Brush your teeth? *1 to 5 gallons*
- Wash the car? 50 *gallons or more*
- Run the washing machine? *34 to 55 gallons (every load)*
- Flush the toilet? *1.5 to 4 gallons (every flush)*

Tips for Conserving Water and Avoiding Pollution

- Water is a very important resource. Try not to use more of it than you need for the task at hand.
- Fix your dripping faucets with new washers. A dripping faucet can waste up to 2,500 gallons of water per year.
- Before running the clothes washer or dishwasher, ask your family to wait until there is a full load in the machine.
- Take short showers. Replace your showerhead with a low-flow version that uses less water.
- When taking a bath, use just the amount of water you need. Do not fill the tub all the way. Try not to let too much excess water run down the drain.
- Did you ever consider reusing water? You might be able to give outdoor plants a drink with your bathwater in the summertime.
- Instead of letting the faucet run to cool the water before you drink, keep your drinking water in the refrigerator.
- Use a broom to clean the driveway instead of squirting it with the hose.
- Tell people not to dump leftover oil, grease, or gasoline on the ground or down a sewer drain. These things can eventually work their way into creeks or rivers.
- When fertilizing your lawn, follow the instructions on the bag of fertilizer. Avoid using more fertilizer than you need for the job. Consider using organic fertilizer.
- Use laundry detergents that are safe for the environment.
- Do not pollute water (lakes and streams) with trash such as cans, bottles, or paper.
- Avoid letting the water run while brushing your teeth or washing your hands.
- Avoid washing dishes under a running faucet. Instead, fill the sink with soapy water.
- Use outdoor plants that do not require much water.
- Water your lawn at night or early in the morning when it is less likely to evaporate before it soaks into the ground.

Glossary

agricultural map: a map that gives information related to farms and farming

agriculture: the work of raising crops and livestock (farm animals)

boundaries: lines on a map that indicate where a country, state, or county ends and another begins

butte: an isolated hill with steep sides that is smaller than a mesa

canyon: a valley with very steep, rocky sides

capital: city where elected officials meet to govern a state or nation

capital resources: things people make and use to make other goods or to provide services

cardinal directions: the four main directions (north, south, east, and west)

cartographer: someone who creates maps

city: a large, densely populated urban area

cliff: a steep, high face of rock

colony: a community of people who settle far from their home but stay in touch with their homeland

community: a place where people live and work together

compass rose: a map symbol that shows directions

condensation: the gathering of water vapor into clouds

consumers: organisms that cannot make their own food and must eat other organisms

continent: one of the seven large landmasses on Earth

coordinate: the place where a line of latitude and a line of longitude meet

country: the territory occupied by a nation

county: a local area within a state

county road: road maintained by a county

cove: a dish-shaped water form, like a small bay, in a lake or ocean

D

dam: a barrier that holds back flowing river water

decomposers: organisms, such as bacteria and worms, that eat decaying matter

desert: a large, dry region that receives little rain

E

economy: the combined business and work done by a community

elevation: the height of land above sea level

equator: an imaginary line drawn around the center of Earth

eruption: a violent explosion from a volcano

evaporation: the process of liquid water turning into water vapor

F

food chain: a diagram showing how each living organism needs other organisms for food

forest: an area dominated by trees and other woody plants

frontier: the far edge of a country, where few people live

G

geography: the study of Earth in all its variety

glacier: a large, slowly moving mass of ice

globe: a model of Earth that is round like a ball

good: a product that can satisfy people's wants and needs

gridlines: the horizontal and vertical lines printed on a map that you can use to find a specific place

H

habitat: the places where animals or plants live

harvest: to gather crops from the fields

hemisphere: *half of a globe,* Earth divided into eastern and western or northern and southern halves

hill: a raised landform that is higher than the surrounding land but is smaller than a mountain

historical map: a map that shows the way places were in the past

homogenization: a process used to prevent the milk fat from separating out of milk products

human resources: people who do the work in an economy

immigrant: someone who leaves one country to live in another

index: a list of the names of places located on the map

intermediate directions: directions, such as northwest or southeast, that are halfway between the cardinal directions

interstate highway: a large highway that links major cities throughout the United States

island: a landmass that is completely surrounded by water

lake: a body of water surrounded by land

landform: the shape, form, or nature of a specific physical feature of Earth's surface, such as a plain, hill, plateau, or mountain

latitude lines: imaginary lines drawn parallel to the equator

legend: a small table that includes every symbol shown on a map and a short description of the feature that the symbol stands for; sometimes called a *map key*

location: the place where something is

longitude lines: imaginary lines drawn parallel to the prime meridian

magma: molten rock within a volcano

manufacturing: the building of products, like cars, televisions, or shoes, for others to buy

map: a drawing of a part of Earth's surface drawn to scale as seen from above

mental map: a way of organizing information in your mind

mesa: a high area of land with a flat top and sides that are usually steep cliffs; smaller than a plateau

mountains: rugged landforms that rise much higher than the surrounding land

mouth: the place where a river empties into another body of water

national park: an area of land set aside by an act of Congress because of its unique physical and/or cultural value to the nation

natural resources: things that occur in nature and are useful to humans, such as water, land, forests, fish, wildlife, and minerals

navigation: (1) ship traffic on a waterway; (2) finding one's way on a journey

neighborhood: a smaller community inside a larger city

nomadic: having the characteristic of moving often from place to place, usually relating to human beings

North Pole: the most northern point on Earth

ocean: one of the four largest bodies of water on Earth that surround the seven continents

organism: a living thing

pasteurization: the process of heating milk to kill the germs it may have

peninsula: a landform that extends into a body of water, with water on three sides

physical map: a map showing Earth's different landforms and water forms

Pilgrims: people who came to America from England in search of religious freedom

plateau: a high area of flat land

point: a landform that extends into a body of water and is smaller than a peninsula

pollution: something that has become unclean or spoiled, usually by waste

port: a place located on a body of water that can receive ships and transfer cargo to and from them

prairie: a treeless, grassy plain

precipitation: liquid or solid water that falls from the atmosphere to Earth

prime meridian: an imaginary line around Earth from top to bottom that runs through the city of Greenwich, England

producers: (1) workers who use resources to make goods or provide services; (2) organisms, like plants, that make their own food

recreation: activities, such as fishing, hiking, or swimming, that people do for fun in their spare time

reservoir: a human-made lake

river: a large, natural stream of water; larger than a creek

rural area: sparsely settled places away from urban areas

scale: the relationship between a certain distance on the map and a distance on the ground

service: something that is done to benefit others; an activity or action that satisfies people's wants or needs

source: the place where a river begins

South Pole: the most southern point on Earth

state: an area within a country that has definite political boundaries and an organized government

state road: a road maintained by a state

suburban area: a community located near or just outside a city

symbols: drawings, lines, or dots that stand for something else

town: an urban area that is smaller than a city

transportation: the many ways of moving people and things from place to place

tributary: a smaller stream that joins a bigger river

urban: a densely populated area with a population of 50,000 or more

U.S. highway: a highway usually maintained by the federal government that allows travel from one state to another

valley: a low-lying area of land, usually containing a river and surrounded by higher areas, such as mountains or hills

volcano: a landform, usually a mountain, where magma erupts through the surface of Earth

water cycle: the continual process of evaporation, condensation, and precipitation

water form: the shape, form, or nature of a specific physical feature of water on Earth, such as a river, lake, or ocean

wetlands: land that is usually wet or flooded much of the year

Index

Greenwich, England, 82
gridlines, 14–17, 19, 84–85

habitat, 86–87
hail, 68–69
harvest, 57
hemispheres, 82–83
highways, 64–65, 100
hills, 34–35
historical map, 51
Hopi, 33
human resources, 54–55

immigrant, 76–78
index, map, 15–16, 19
Indian Ocean, 2–3, 83, 98
Indian Territory, Oklahoma, 46–47
intermediate directions, 14–15
interstate highways, 64–65
island, 76–77

Jackson, Wyoming, 26

Kentucky Lake, 43, 105
key, map, 10

labor, 54–55
lakes, 34–35, 38–40, 73, 105
landforms, 3, 32–37, 100
latitude, 82–85
Laurens County, South Carolina, 64–65
Lawton, Oklahoma, 22–23
legend, map, 4, 10–11, 13–15, 17–19, 88–89
lobster fishing, 80–81
locations, 14–15
longitude, 82–85

magma, 32
Maine, 27, 30–31, 80–81, 84–85, 103
manufacturing, 20
map, 14–15

agricultural, 58–59
city park, 88–89
climate, 100
economic or resource, 100
historical, 51
mental, 9, 12–13
movement of people, 46–47
physical, 3–5, 100
political, 100
precipitation, 70–71
river, 40–41
road, 64–65, 100
state, 28–31, 36–37, 84–85
topographic, 100
map grid, 14–17, 19, 84–85
map index, 15–16, 19
map key, 10
map scale, 15, 22–23
map symbols, 14–15, 18–19, 88–89, 100
map title, 14–15
Marietta, Ohio, 20–21, 24–25
Massachusetts, 50–51
Mayflower, 50–51
mental map, 9, 12–13
meridians, 82–83
mesa, 33, 34–37
milk, 57–59
mountains, 3–5, 26, 32–37
Mount St. Helens, 32–33
mouth, river, 38, 41, 43
Muskingum River, 20–21

national park, 28–29
Native Americans, 33, 44–49
natural resources, 44, 51–54
Navajo, 33
navigation, 39
neighborhood, 8, 12–13, 74–75, 78–79
Nickajack Lake, 43, 105
nomadic, 45
North America, 2–3, 9, 94–95, 98
North Dakota, 70–71
North Pole, 2, 4–5, 82

oceans, 2–5, 7, 83, 98
Ohio River, 20–21, 38, 41
Oklahoma, 22–23, 46–47
Old Town, Maine, 27
organism, 87, 90–91
Ozarks, 26–27

Answer Key

Page 4

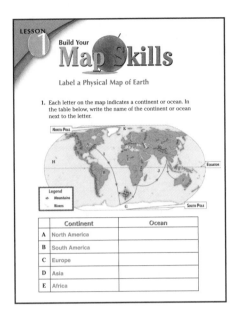

LESSON 1
Build Your Map Skills

Label a Physical Map of Earth

1. Each letter on the map indicates a continent or ocean. In the table below, write the name of the continent or ocean next to the letter.

	Continent	Ocean
A	North America	
B	South America	
C	Europe	
D	Asia	
E	Africa	

Page 5

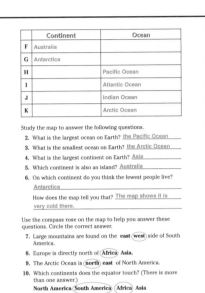

	Continent	Ocean
F	Australia	
G	Antarctica	
H		Pacific Ocean
I		Atlantic Ocean
J		Indian Ocean
K		Arctic Ocean

Study the map to answer the following questions.

2. What is the largest ocean on Earth? the Pacific Ocean
3. What is the smallest ocean on Earth? the Arctic Ocean
4. What is the largest continent on Earth? Asia
5. Which continent is also an island? Australia
6. On which continent do you think the fewest people live? Antarctica
   How does the map tell you that? The map shows it is very cold there.

Use the compass rose on the map to help you answer these questions. Circle the correct answer.

7. Large mountains are found on the **east** (**west**) side of South America.
8. Europe is directly north of (**Africa**) Asia.
9. The Arctic Ocean is (**north**) **east** of North America.
10. Which continents does the equator touch? (There is more than one answer.)
    North America (**South America**) (**Africa**) Asia

Page 6

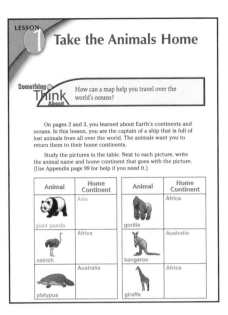

LESSON 1
Take the Animals Home

Something to Think About
How can a map help you travel over the world's oceans?

On pages 2 and 3, you learned about Earth's continents and oceans. In this lesson, you are the captain of a ship that is full of lost animals from all over the world. The animals want you to return them to their home continents.

Study the pictures in the table. Next to each picture, write the animal name and home continent that goes with the picture. (Use Appendix page 99 for help if you need it.)

Animal	Home Continent	Animal	Home Continent
giant panda	Asia	gorilla	Africa
ostrich	Africa	kangaroo	Australia
platypus	Australia	giraffe	Africa

Page 7

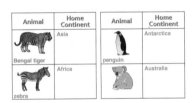

Animal	Home Continent	Animal	Home Continent
Bengal tiger	Asia	penguin	Antarctica
zebra	Africa	koala	Australia

Use the world map on page 4 to navigate the world's oceans to take the animals home. As you work through the questions, draw a line to each continent with a colored pencil.

1. From the star on the map, draw your route to Antarctica. Which animal will you take to Antarctica? penguin
   In which direction will you travel to get there? south
2. From Antarctica, draw your route to Africa. Which animals will you take to Africa? zebra, giraffe, ostrich, gorilla
   Through which ocean will you travel? Atlantic Ocean
3. From Africa, draw your route to Asia. Which animals will you take to Asia? Bengal tiger, giant panda
   In which general direction will you travel to get there? northeast
4. From Asia, draw your route to Australia. Which animals will you take to Australia? kangaroo, platypus, koala
   Through which ocean will you travel? Indian Ocean

Page 10

LESSON 2
Build Your Map Skills

Follow Map Directions

You can use a map to help you find where things are and to get from place to place. Most maps include a compass rose and a legend, or map key.

A **legend** will show you what different symbols on a map mean. It is a small table that includes every symbol shown on a map. The legend describes the feature that each symbol or color stands for. If you are looking for a park on a map, for example, find the symbol in the legend that means *park*. Then, find that symbol on the map.

At the beginning of this lesson, you read about Taylor Anderson and her many places in the world. One of these places is the town of Pine Lake. Use this map of Pine Lake to answer the questions.

1. Follow the bike path to the school from Taylor's house. What important places does she pass?
   the town hall, police station, and fire station
2. Name two streets in Pine Lake that run north and south. Possible answer: Long Street and Short Street
3. Which buildings are located on the corner of Main Street and Long Street? the fire station and police station
4. Describe one route Taylor could use to walk to school each day. Possible answer: Taylor could walk west on Pell Street and then turn north (right) on Long Street.
5. Suppose Taylor is at Pine Lake Mall. What street is she on? Ash Street

Page 11

6. Describe a route she could take to get home from Pine Lake Mall. Possible answer: She could walk west on Ash Street to the bike path. She could follow the bike path south along Elk River. She should cross the river on the bridge near her house. The bike path continues west right past her house.
7. What is the name of the river that lies east of Taylor's house? Elk River

Answer Key

Draw a Mental Map

Something to Think About

How do people find their way when they go from place to place?

People often use a mental map to get from place to place. A mental map is your idea of where you are. A mental map should include buildings and places.

Think about the places you often go in your community. You may go to the post office to mail letters. You may go to the grocery store to buy food.

On pages 10 and 11, you worked with a simple map of Taylor Anderson's community. You learned how to locate important places and how to use a map to get from one place to another. In this activity, you will make a simple mental map of your own neighborhood or community.

1. Write your complete address, including your town or city, your state, and your ZIP code.
   Answers will vary.

2. Make a list of some of the important places close to where you live (for example, your home, school, post office, grocery store, or friends' homes).
   Answers will vary.

12

---

3. Are there any other important features near your home such as parks, lakes, or rivers?
   Answers will vary.

4. What are the names of some important streets or highways in your community?
   Answers will vary.

5. Think for a moment about the important places you named in question 2. Picture your home first. Then, think of where the other places are compared to where your home is located. On a separate piece of paper, draw a mental map of your neighborhood or community. Use the map of Pine Lake on page 11 as a model for your map.

6. Next to your map, make a simple legend, like the one on page 11. The map legends will vary.

7. Now, use the map you have created to plan a route from your home to a place in your community. Use the space below to describe your route. For example, your trip could be to school, to a park, or to a friend's house. Be sure to name the streets you need to use and the directions you need to travel to get where you are going.

When you finish, ask an adult to check your mental map and the route you planned. If you need to, walk through your neighborhood and make corrections.
Answers will vary.

13

Build Your Map Skills

Use a Map Grid

Your cousin Mark is visiting from out of town and wants you to help him find his way around. You will use this map of your town to help him locate the places he wants to visit.

1. Name two fun and interesting places Mark might like to visit that are on Orange Road. What are their grid locations?
   E4: History Museum E7: Shopping Mall

2. Give directions for the best way for Mark to get from the library to city hall. From the library, follow Brown Street east and turn right on Palmer Street. Turn right on Ellis Road and then left on Orange Road.

3. Mark wants to know if there are any parks in town. Are there? Name the park and its grid reference.
   Big Bay Park is at B6.

4. In the space below, create an index for this map. Each place in the index needs a grid reference number.

Map Index	Grid Number
Big Bay Harbor	B7
City Hall	F5
High School	C3
History Museum	E4
Library	C2
Post Office	F3
Shopping Mall	E7

16

---

5. From the park, Mark would like to ride his bike. Which direction does the bike path run? West
   The path runs along what creek? Lost Creek

6. Mark wants to mail some postcards to his friends back home. What is the grid reference for the post office? F3

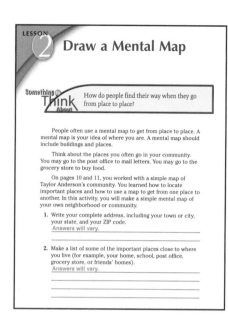

17

Make a Map with a Legend

Something to Think About

How do you use the features of a map?

A **cartographer** is someone who creates maps. In this lesson, you will be a cartographer and make a map of your town. You will create a legend with symbols for buildings, parks, and other landmarks. You will also create a grid, index, and compass rose so people can find things on the map easily. You can use the map on page 15 as a guide to help you make your map.

1. Name at least five important places in your town or community, like a school, a park, or a shopping mall. Write their names in the table below. Name more if you want to. Include notes about the location of each place.

2. Next to each place you listed, draw a symbol you will use to stand for it on your map. Use different colors for the symbols you create.

Important Places	Location	Symbol
Answers will vary.		

18

---

3. Name at least five streets to include on your map. Next to each street name, write the direction it runs. Ask an adult for help with the directions if you are not sure.

Street Name	Direction
Answers will vary.	

4. Now, get a large sheet of paper to draw your map. First, draw a compass rose in one of the corners. Then, draw lines on the map to show the streets you named in question 3. Draw the streets in the correct location and direction. Write the name of the streets on the map.

5. It is time to add the places you named in question 1 to the map. Use the symbols you created and put them on the correct streets.

6. Now, use a ruler to mark off gridlines on your map. Measure carefully to space the gridlines the same distance apart. Label the vertical gridlines with numbers at the top of your map. Label the horizontal gridlines with letters at the side of your map.

7. Create a map legend, using the symbols you created for the places on your map.

8. Finally, create a map index by listing the names and grid reference numbers of each place on your map.

19

Answer Key

Page 22

LESSON 4

Build Your Map Skills

Use a Compass Rose and Scale

A map scale helps you tell how far away one place is from another. For this lesson, you will learn how to measure distance in air miles. To do this, mark the length of the scale on a piece of paper. Track the distance across the map with the scale. Multiply to figure the distance in miles.

Police officers provide lots of important services to their community. In this activity, you will be a police officer in Lawton, Oklahoma. Remember to take the shortest route as you travel.

What things does a police officer do to help people?

1. In your police car, you are passing the golf course headed east on W Gore Blvd. A motorist on NW 38th St. near Greer Park needs help changing a flat tire. Describe how to get to the motorist. About how far will you need to travel?
   I need to continue traveling east and then I should turn north on NW 38th St. I need to travel about 1 mile to Greer Park.

2. You get a call about a traffic accident at the corner of NW Cache Rd. and NW Sheridan Rd. Describe how you will get there from Greer Park.
   From Greer Park, I will go north on NW 38th St. I will turn east on NW Cache Rd. and follow it to NW Sheridan Rd.

Page 23

3. You are at Comanche Hospital. There is a lost boy at Fred Bently Park who needs help getting home. About how far are you from this park? Which direction will you travel to get there?
   I am about ¾ of a mile from Fred Bently Park. To get there, I will travel west on W Gore Blvd. and turn right (north) on NW 40th St. I will then turn left (west) on NW Columbia Ave. to the park.

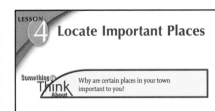

LAWTON, OKLAHOMA

Legend			
N	North	SW	Southwest
S	South	NE	Northeast
E	East	SE	Southeast
W	West	Blvd.	Boulevard
NW	Northwest	St.	Street

Page 24

LESSON 4

Locate Important Places

Something to Think About

Why are certain places in your town important to you?

People in Marietta, Ohio, use their knowledge of important places and landmarks to help them get from one location to another. Use the map on page 21 to learn about important places in Marietta, Ohio.

1. In the left column of the table below is a list of important places or landmarks on the map of Marietta. In the right column, describe where these places are. The first item has been completed for you.

Important Places in Marietta, Ohio	
Important Places	**Location Description**
Muskingum River	The Muskingum River flows southeast through town between Gilman Street and Front Street. It flows into the Ohio River.
Fort Harmar Historical Village	Maple and Gilman Streets
Post Office	Front Street near Union Street
Marietta College	4th Street and Putnam Street
Lafayette Hotel	2nd and OH-7, near the Ohio River

Page 25

Refer to pages 20–21 and answer these questions about the community of Marietta, Ohio.

2. When was Marietta founded? Who founded the city?
   Marietta was founded in 1788 by a group of 47 pioneers who arrived where the Muskingum and Ohio rivers come together.

3. Why is Marietta's location on two rivers important to the community?
   The rivers helped the city become an early center of manufacturing, making it easier for the people of Marietta to ship their goods to customers.

4. There are many important places in your community. What do people at these places do for the community to make it better? Use the table below to describe important places in your community. Use a separate piece of paper, if necessary.

Important Places in Your Community	
Important Places	**Why Is This Place Important?**
Hospital	Answers will vary.
Library	
School	
Police Station	
Other:	

What happens at a school that makes it an important place?

Page 29

Answer the questions below to learn more about communities within the state of Wyoming.

1. In what part of the state is Wyoming's capital city located?
   the southeast

2. With which states does Wyoming share a border? (See Appendix page 98 for a key to state abbreviations.)
   Montana, Idaho, Utah, Colorado, Nebraska, and South Dakota

3. What are the names of the national parks shown on the map?
   Yellowstone National Park and Grand Teton National Park

4. What is the name of the river that flows past Casper, Wyoming? North Platte River

5. According to the map, near which cities is skiing popular?
   Cody, Jackson, and Rawlins

6. Name two reservoirs shown on the map.
   Possible answer: Boyson Reservoir and Flaming Gorge Reservoir

7. Look on Appendix page 101 for population information for the Wyoming communities shown on the map. List them below from the largest to the smallest based on their population. Cheyenne, Casper, Laramie, Gillette, Rock Springs, Sheridan, Green River, Cody, Jackson, Rawlins

The state government is located in Cheyenne, the capital.

Page 30

LESSON 5

Make a State Vacation Guide

Something to Think About

Why are physical features of communities important?

In this activity, you will learn about the physical features of communities within a state. You will use facts about these places to create a vacation guide to attract people to visit there.

Refer again to pages 26–27, which describe both Arkansas and Maine. Study the maps of Arkansas and Maine on the next page. Choose one of these two states, and then answer the questions to help you plan your vacation guide. Use a separate piece of paper, if you need more room.

1. List some important physical features of the state you chose. You could include rivers, lakes, mountains, the coast, or other features in your list. Answers will vary.

2. List things to do in the state that might be fun or educational for visitors. Make notes about why these activities would be fun or educational. Answers will vary.

3. On a separate piece of paper, create a vacation guide for the state. Paste or tape pictures onto your vacation guide from magazines or newspapers. You should include at least one picture and a description of what makes the state a great place to visit. Use all the information you have put together to help create your vacation guide.

Answer Key

Page 35

Identify the landforms and water forms on the map by writing their names in the blank spaces. When you are done, answer the questions below.

1. How are a plateau, a mesa, and a butte different from one another? **A plateau covers a wider area than a mesa or a butte. A mesa is not as wide as a plateau, but it is wider than a butte.**

2. How are valleys and canyons the same? **Both valleys and canyons have high areas and low areas of land, so a river often runs through the center of a valley or canyon.**

3. How is a lake different than a river? **A river contains water that flows. The water remains generally still within a lake.**

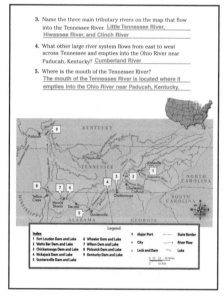

mountain, volcano, cliff, valley, lake, hill, river, mesa, desert, plateau, canyon, butte

35

Page 36

Landforms and Water Forms of Arizona

Something to Think About: Why are landforms and water forms shown on a map?

Complete the table below by referring to the map of Arizona on page 37. The first item has been completed for you as an example. Possible answers are listed below. There may be other correct answers.

Landform or Water Form Types	Landform Example from Map of Arizona	Location of Landform within Arizona
butte	Hopi Buttes	northeast of Winslow at the edge of the Painted Desert
canyon	Grand Canyon	north central Arizona, north of the Coconino Plateau
cliffs	Grand Wash Cliffs	in northwest Arizona, north of Kingman
desert	Painted Desert	northeast of Winslow and Flagstaff
plateau	Kaibito Plateau	in northern Arizona, northwest of Black Mesa
river	Gila River	in southwestern Arizona, between Phoenix and Yuma
mesa	Black Mesa	in northeastern Arizona, northeast of Flagstaff
mountains	Castle Dome Mountains	in southwestern Arizona, north of Yuma

36

Page 37

Answer the questions below.

1. What river runs through the city of Tucson? **Santa Cruz River**

2. Which river runs near the city of Winslow? **the Little Colorado River**

3. In what part of Arizona are most of the deep canyons and high mesas, buttes, and plateaus located? **in the northern part of the state**

4. Bill Williams was a famous mountain man in the region. Describe the location of the river that was named for him. **Bill Williams River is in the west central part of the state, south of the Hualapai Mountains.**

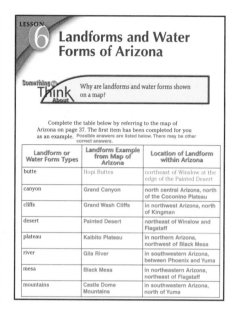

37

Page 40

Build Your Map Skills

Reading a River Map

Look at the map and read again about the Tennessee River on pages 38–39. Then, answer the questions below.

1. The Tennessee River officially begins one mile above Knoxville, Tennessee. Name the states through which the Tennessee River flows. **Tennessee, Alabama, Mississippi, and Kentucky**

2. Complete the table below about the lakes on the Tennessee River. (Two of the lakes extend into more than one state.)

Dam	Name of Lake	States
Pickwick Dam	Pickwick Lake	Alabama, Mississippi, and Tennessee
Watts Bar Dam	Watts Bar Lake	Tennessee
Fort Loudon Dam	Fort Loudon Lake	Tennessee
Nickajack Dam	Nickajack Lake	Tennessee
Wilson Dam	Wilson Lake	Alabama
Wheeler Dam	Wheeler Lake	Alabama
Chickamauga Dam	Chickamauga Lake	Tennessee
Guntersville Dam	Guntersville Lake	Alabama
Kentucky Dam	Kentucky Lake	Tennessee, Kentucky

40

Page 41

3. Name the three main tributary rivers on the map that flow into the Tennessee River. **Little Tennessee River, Hiwassee River, and Clinch River**

4. What other large river system flows from east to west across Tennessee and empties into the Ohio River near Paducah, Kentucky? **Cumberland River**

5. Where is the mouth of the Tennessee River? **The mouth of the Tennessee River is located where it empties into the Ohio River near Paducah, Kentucky.**

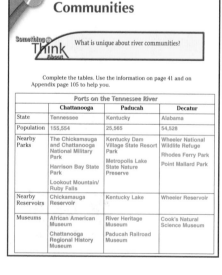

41

Page 42

Learn about River Communities

Something to Think About: What is unique about river communities?

Complete the tables. Use the information on page 41 and on Appendix page 105 to help you.

Ports on the Tennessee River			
	Chattanooga	Paducah	Decatur
State	Tennessee	Kentucky	Alabama
Population	155,554	25,565	54,528
Nearby Parks	The Chickamauga and Chattanooga National Military Park; Harrison Bay State Park; Lookout Mountain/ Ruby Falls	Kentucky Dam Village State Resort Park; Metropolis Lake State Nature Preserve	Wheeler National Wildlife Refuge; Rhodes Ferry Park; Point Mallard Park
Nearby Reservoirs	Chickamauga Reservoir	Kentucky Lake	Wheeler Reservoir
Museums	African American Museum; Chattanooga Regional History Museum	River Heritage Museum; Paducah Railroad Museum	Cook's Natural Science Museum

42

Answer Key

Page 43

Reservoirs on the Tennessee River

	Kentucky	Nickajack	Pickwick	Watts Bar
Length of shoreline (miles)	2,380	215	496	783
Size (acres)	160,000	10,370	43,100	39,000
Year completed	1944	1967	1938	1942

Use information from pages 38–39 to answer the following questions.

1. What is a port? A port is a place located on a river or lake that can receive ships and transfer cargo to and from them.

2. What is a reservoir? A reservoir is a lake made when human beings dam a river.

3. Name one way that water is used from the reservoirs on the Tennessee River. Possible answer: for drinking water

4. What is the difference between a river's source and a river's mouth? The source is where the river begins. The mouth is where the river empties into another body of water, such as another river or a lake.

5. Why is recreation important to businesses in Tennessee? People having fun spend money that creates jobs in the state of Tennessee.

6. Refer to the list of rivers on Appendix page 104. What are the four longest rivers in the United States? the Missouri River, the Mississippi River, the Yukon River, and the Rio Grande River

7. How long is the Tennessee River? The Tennessee River is about 886 miles long.

43

Page 47

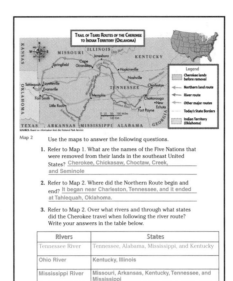

Map 2

Use the maps to answer the following questions.

1. Refer to Map 1. What are the names of the Five Nations that were removed from their lands in the southeast United States? Cherokee, Chickasaw, Choctaw, Creek, and Seminole

2. Refer to Map 2. Where did the Northern Route begin and end? It began near Charleston, Tennessee, and it ended at Tahlequah, Oklahoma.

3. Refer to Map 2. Over what rivers and through what states did the Cherokee travel when following the river route? Write your answers in the table below.

Rivers	States
Tennessee River	Tennessee, Alabama, Mississippi, and Kentucky
Ohio River	Kentucky, Illinois
Mississippi River	Missouri, Arkansas, Kentucky, Tennessee, and Mississippi
Arkansas River	Arkansas

47

Page 48

LESSON 8
Learn More about Native Americans

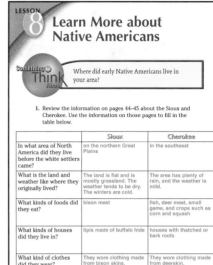

Something to Think About Where did early Native Americans live in your area?

1. Review the information on pages 44–45 about the Sioux and Cherokee. Use the information on those pages to fill in the table below.

	Sioux	Cherokee
In what area of North America did they live before the white settlers came?	on the northern Great Plains	in the southeast
What is the land and weather like where they originally lived?	The land is flat and is mostly grassland. The weather tends to be dry. The winters are cold.	The area has plenty of rain, and the weather is mild.
What kinds of foods did they eat?	bison meat	fish, deer meat, small game, and crops such as corn and squash
What kinds of houses did they live in?	tipis made of buffalo hide	houses with thatched or bark roofs
What kind of clothes did they wear?	They wore clothing made from bison skins.	They wore clothing made from deerskin.

48

Page 49

For the next activity, you will do some research in the library or in books you may have. If you need to, ask an adult for help finding some of the information.

2. Find out about the lives of the Sioux and Cherokee people today. Use the information you find to fill in the table.

	Sioux	Cherokee
Where do they live today?	Today, most of the Sioux live on reservations in South Dakota, North Dakota, Montana, and Nebraska.	Today, most of the Cherokee live on reservations in North Carolina and Oklahoma.
What kinds of jobs do they have today?	Possible Answer: Many Sioux have had to move to cities to find work. Like other Americans, these Sioux work at all kinds of jobs. Sioux on the reservations may be farmers, cattle ranchers, hunting guides, or may run other businesses.	Possible Answer: Cherokee run a variety of businesses on and near their reservation lands. For example, on the Oklahoma reservation, they run a golf course. The reservation in North Carolina has a variety of businesses related to tourism.
What kinds of houses do they live in today?	The Sioux generally live in the same types of houses and apartments as other Americans.	Cherokee generally live in the same types of houses and apartments as other Americans.

3. Find out about a Native American community in or near your state. Write what you learn in the table.

What is the name of the Native American community?	Answers will vary.
Where did these people live in the past? Where do they live today?	Answers will vary.
How did they use the land in the past? What kinds of jobs do they have today?	Answers will vary.

49

Page 52

LESSON 9
Build Your Map Skills

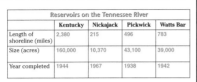

Learn about the Economy of the 13 Colonies

The business and work done by people in a community is called an **economy**. Natural resources are very important to most economies. For example, wood from trees is a natural resource. People in the American Colonies used wood to make tables and chairs. They then sold the tables and chairs to other people in the community.

The people of Plymouth Colony learned how to use the natural resources around them in order to live. Other settlers who formed colonies in America also used natural resources in their economies. Different colonies became good at making and growing different things. They traded and sold these products to make money.

The map shows some of the products made and sold by the 13 colonies. Look at the map and answer the following questions.

1. Name the Northern Colonies shown on the map. New Hampshire, Massachusetts, Rhode Island, and Connecticut

2. Name the Middle Colonies. New York, Pennsylvania, New Jersey, and Delaware

3. Name the Southern Colonies. Virginia, Maryland, North Carolina, South Carolina, and Georgia

4. According to the map, were ships made in the Northern, Middle, or Southern colonies? Ships were made in the Northern and Middle colonies.

52

Page 53

5. In which colonies was tobacco grown? Delaware, Maryland, Virginia, and North Carolina

6. What products were produced in South Carolina and Georgia that were not produced in the Northern Colonies? indigo, rice, and cotton

7. In which colonies was trapping important? Georgia, North Carolina, Pennsylvania, and New York

8. Name three colonies that probably had large forests. How do you know? Possible answer: Massachusetts, New York, and North Carolina probably had large forests. I know this because the map shows that lumber was an important product in these colonies.

53

Answer Key

Picture 1   Picture 2   Picture 3

1. Look at Picture 1, which shows a painter painting a house. Who is the producer in the picture? What tools does he use to do the job? The painter painting the house is the producer. He uses a paint brush and a ladder.

Is the painter providing a good or a service?
The painter is providing a service.

2. Look at Picture 2. Is the barber making a good or providing a service for the boy? What tools does he use?
The barber is providing a service. The barber uses scissors to cut hair and a special chair for the boy to sit in.

3. Look at Picture 3, which shows a worker building a car. Is this worker making a good or providing a service?—the worker is making a good—the car.

4. In the table, write the names of two adults you know and the work they do to make a living. Write whether they produce mostly goods or services.

Names of Adults	What They Do	Goods or Services?
Answers will vary.		

55

Build Your Map Skills

Use an Agricultural Map

As you have already learned, farm crops are grown and animals are raised on farms all over the United States. The type of farm products that can be produced in each area of the country depends upon the weather, rainfall, and type of soil in that area.

An **agricultural map** gives information related to farms and farming. For example, it can show the number of farms in a state or the type of crops that farmers grow. Map 1 shows the number of milk cows in each state in the United States. Map 2 shows the number of milk cows in each county of the state of Pennsylvania. (A county is a local area within a state.)

Use Map 1 to answer the following questions.

1. Which five states have the most milk cows?
New York, Pennsylvania, Wisconsin, Minnesota, and California

2. According to Map 1, most states have about how many milk cows?
400,000 or less

3. Which state has more milk cows, California or Minnesota?
California has more milk cows than Minnesota.

Use Map 2 to answer the following questions.

4. Which five counties in Pennsylvania have the most milk cows? What cities and towns are located in those counties? Write this information in the table.

58

County	Cities and Towns
Bradford	Troy, Rome
Berks	Reading
Lancaster	Lancaster
Lebanon	Richland
Franklin	Chambersburg

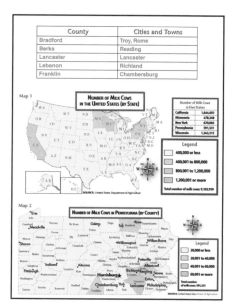

59

Agriculture in Your State

Something to Think About   Why are farms and farmers important?

In this lesson, you have learned about many types of farm products. Have you ever thought about what farm products might be grown or made near your community? Do the farms near where you live produce different kinds of products?

1. What farm crops are grown in your state or near your community? Answers will vary.

2. What farm animals are raised in your state or near your community? Answers will vary.

3. Visit a local grocery store and ask to talk to the store manager. Ask if the store sells any farm products that are grown or raised locally. If so, list them. Answers will vary.

Find out how farm life has changed over the past 50 years. Talk to relatives or neighbors who grew up on farms. Ask them the following questions, and write down the answers.

4. Where was the farm where you grew up? Answers will vary.

60

---

5. What was farm life like? How was it different than your life now? Answers will vary.

6. What farm products did your farm produce? Answers will vary.

7. List two of your favorite foods in the table below. Find out where these foods come from—do they come from a plant or an animal? How are they grown or made?

Favorite Food	Where is it grown or made? How is it processed?
	Answers will vary.

Wool is from the outer coat of sheep. It is processed and dyed (colored) to make yarn and other products.

61

Build Your Map Skills

Use a County Road Map

The map on the next page shows Laurens County in the state of South Carolina. A **county** is a local area with political boundaries within a state. Most states have many counties.

The **interstate highways** shown on the map are part of a larger network of roads connecting cities and states all over the country. They may have two, three, or even four lanes going both ways. There are no traffic lights on interstate highways.

U.S. highways are usually smaller than interstate highways. They are more often two-lane roads. These highways also allow travel from one state to another. A **state** or **county** road is usually a two-lane road.

Use the map to answer the questions below.

1. Start at the far western corner of the county (near Princeton). From there, measure to the far eastern corner of the county. About how far is it? Use the map scale. Write the distance below.
about 37 miles

2. Start at the northwest corner of Laurens County (north of Fountain Inn). Measure to the southeast corner of the county (southeast of Cross Hill). About how far is it? Write the distance below.
about 40 miles

3. Name two interstate highways that run through Laurens County. In what direction do they run?
Interstate highways 26 and 385 run from the southeast to the northwest across Laurens County.

64

Answer Key

4. Describe what roads you would use to get from Gray Court to Princeton. Use the compass rose to describe the directions you would travel.
I would take State/County Road 101 southwest and then south to Hickory Tavern. I would then turn right (west) on to U.S. Highway 76 to Princeton.

5. Describe how you would travel from the town of Clinton to Cross Hill.
I would take State/County Road 72 southwest from Clinton to Cross Hill.

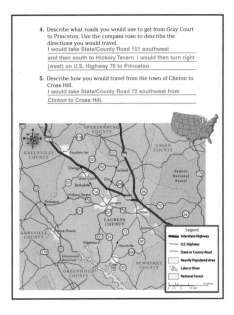

65

LESSON 11

Transportation in Your Town

Something to Think About
What is so important about the transportation of people and things?

1. Write down three methods of transportation in your town. Describe how each method of transportation gets people from place to place.

Method of transportation	How does it move people and things?
bicycle	It moves mostly people, usually along a road or pathway. A few items can be stored in a basket or saddle bags.
Answers will vary.	

66

---

2. Ask three adults how they get to work each day. What type of transportation do they use? What route do they take to get to work? Write your answers below.

Name	Type of Transportation	Route to Work
Jason	Bus	north on the circle freeway
Answers will vary.		

3. Using magazines and newspapers, find some pictures of products being transported in several different ways. These methods of transportation could be by train, in trucks or cars, on ships, or any other method of transportation. Cut the pictures out and tape them on a separate piece of paper. Now use the pictures to make up a story about transportation. Your story should answer as many of the questions below as possible. Add any other details that you think are important. Write your story on a separate piece of paper.

What items are being transported? Answers will vary.

Where did the items come from? _____

Where are the items going? _____

How will the items be used? _____

67

LESSON 12

Build Your Map Skills

Reading a Precipitation Map

Different parts of the United States get different amounts of precipitation. Map 1 shows the precipitation received throughout the United States over one year. Map 2 shows the precipitation that falls each year in North Dakota. The amounts on the map are average amounts. That means it rains or snows about that much every year.

Study the maps and answer the following questions.

1. Look at Map 1. Which states in the West get the most precipitation? Write the state names in the space below.
Washington and Oregon

2. On Map 1, which states do you think include desert regions? How do you know? Desert regions are in California, Nevada, and Arizona. I know this because parts of these states get less than 5 inches of rain per year.

3. Study Map 2 and complete the table below.

Cities and Counties in North Dakota	Location within the State	Average Annual Precipitation
Bismarck	Burleigh County	15–20 inches
Bowman County	southwest	15–20 inches
Fargo	Cass County	more than 25 inches
Griggs County	east-central	more than 25 inches

70

LESSON 12

Conserving Water and Keeping It Clean

Something to Think About
How can you help to reduce water pollution?

1. Read the tips on Appendix page 106 about ways to reduce water use and pollution. Complete the table.

Ways to Reduce Water Use	Ways to Reduce Water Pollution
Answers will vary. Any of the tips from the Appendix may be listed.	

2. We all use lots of water every day. Look at Appendix page 106 to find out how much water it takes to do the things listed below.

Daily Activity	Amount of Water Used
washing the car	50 gallons or more
using the dishwasher	7 to 16 gallons
taking a shower	15 to 26 gallons
running the washing machine	34 to 55 gallons

72

---

3. How can you tell if your community has a water pollution problem? Ask a few adults what they know. Read local newspapers or ask your state department of natural resources. Find answers to these questions:
Do fish, frogs, ducks, and other animals live in local lakes and rivers? Are these animals healthy? Answers will vary.

Are the fish caught in local rivers and lakes safe to eat?
Answers will vary.

4. Make a list of animals that live near your community that depend upon clean water. Where do you think these animals find drinking water? Answers will vary.

5. Your water could come from many sources. Your community water department may pump it from wells, from a river, or from a reservoir. Your family may pump water from your own well. Find out where your water comes from. Write what you find out in the space below.
Answers will vary.

6. Try this activity to better understand the water cycle. You will need a large bowl, a mug, some clear plastic wrap, and some water. Take the bowl outside and place it in a sunny spot. Fill it partly full of water and put the empty mug in the center of the bowl. Cover the bowl with plastic wrap. Let the bowl sit in the sun for a couple of hours. The diagram on page 68 will help you understand what happens in the bowl. Write your description in the space below.
Heat from the sun caused the water in the bowl to turn to vapor (called evaporation). The vapor rose to the top of the bowl. There it condensed on the plastic wrap. These droplets gathered and became heavy. They then fell (like rain does) into the mug and bowl.

73

Answer Key

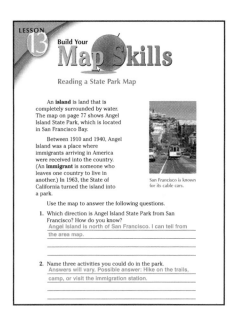

An **island** is land that is completely surrounded by water. The map on page 77 shows Angel Island State Park, which is located in San Francisco Bay.

Between 1910 and 1940, Angel Island was a place where immigrants arriving in America were received into the country. (An **immigrant** is someone who leaves one country to live in another.) In 1963, the State of California turned the island into a park.

San Francisco is known for its cable cars.

Use the map to answer the following questions.

1. Which direction is Angel Island State Park from San Francisco? How do you know?
   Angel Island is north of San Francisco. I can tell from
   the area map.

2. Name three activities you could do in the park.
   Answers will vary. Possible answer: Hike on the trails,
   camp, or visit the immigration station.

76

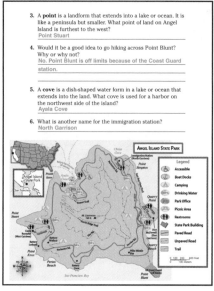

3. A **point** is a landform that extends into a lake or ocean. It is like a peninsula but smaller. What point of land on Angel Island is furthest to the west?
   Point Stuart

4. Would it be a good idea to go hiking across Point Blunt? Why or why not?
   No. Point Blunt is off limits because of the Coast Guard
   station.

5. A **cove** is a dish-shaped water form in a lake or ocean that extends into the land. What cove is used for a harbor on the northwest side of the island?
   Ayala Cove

6. What is another name for the immigration station?
   North Garrison

ANGEL ISLAND STATE PARK

Legend
- Accessible
- Boat Docks
- Camping
- Drinking Water
- Park Office
- Picnic Area
- Restrooms
- State Park Building
- Paved Road
- Unpaved Road
- Trail

77

What Makes a City?

Something to Think About

What makes a community unique?

1. Look again at the material about San Francisco on pages 74–75. Describe three special things about San Francisco.
   Answers will vary. Possible answer: cable cars, the Golden
   Gate Bridge, and the many unique neighborhoods

2. Look closely at the map of San Francisco on page 75. Name three San Francisco neighborhoods.
   Answers will vary.

3. On pages 76–77, you learned about the immigrants who came from far-off countries to Angel Island. Today, many people go to Angel Island State Park each year to visit the immigration station. Why do you think they go there?
   Possible answer: Many people probably want to visit the
   first place where their relatives may have set foot in the
   United States. Others may be interested in the history
   of immigration and the experience of being an immigrant.

4. Use the library to find information about two large communities in your state. Do not use the community you live in. Fill in the table on the next page with the information you find.

78

	Community Name:	Community Name:
Population	Answers will vary.	
Geography (location, climate, nearby landforms and water forms)		
Cultural activities (museums, festivals, theaters, and so on)		
Major businesses and industries		
Fun things to do		

5. Find out if the two communities you have chosen have any special neighborhoods. If so, write their names and describe them on the lines below.
   Answers will vary.

79

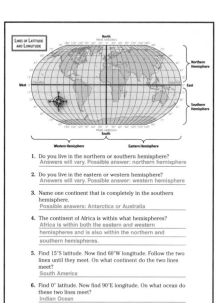

LINES OF LATITUDE AND LONGITUDE

1. Do you live in the northern or southern hemisphere?
   Answers will vary. Possible answer: northern hemisphere

2. Do you live in the eastern or western hemisphere?
   Answers will vary. Possible answer: western hemisphere

3. Name one continent that is completely in the southern hemisphere.
   Possible answers: Antarctica or Australia

4. The continent of Africa is within what hemispheres?
   Africa is within both the eastern and western
   hemispheres and is also within the northern and
   southern hemispheres.

5. Find 15°S latitude. Now find 60°W longitude. Follow the two lines until they meet. On what continent do the two lines meet?
   South America

6. Find 0° latitude. Now find 90°E longitude. On what ocean do these two lines meet?
   Indian Ocean

83

Use a Grid to Find Places on a State Map

Something to Think About

What is the purpose of lines of latitude and longitude?

The map shows the major degrees of latitude and longitude that cross the state of Maine. These lines of latitude and longitude create a grid across the state. The place where a line of latitude and a line of longitude meet is called a **coordinate**.

To better understand this, put a ruler across the map at 47°N latitude and draw a line with a pencil across the state. Now put the ruler across the map at 68°W longitude and draw another line across the state. The place where the two lines meet is the **coordinate** named 47°N latitude, 68°W longitude.

In this activity, you will use lines of latitude and longitude to find places on a state map.

1. Flagstaff Lake is just north of what latitude?
   45°N

2. What city is closest to 47°N latitude and 68°W longitude?
   Caribou

3. What lakes are between 69°N longitude and 70°W longitude?
   Chamberlain, Chesuncook, and Moosehead lakes

4. What city is closest to 45°N latitude and 69°W longitude?
   Bangor

5. Penobscot Bay is at about what grid coordinate?
   44° latitude and 69° longitude

84

Answer Key

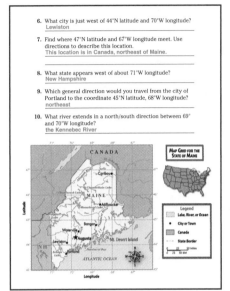

6. What city is just west of 44°N latitude and 70°W longitude?
Lewiston

7. Find where 47°N latitude and 67°W longitude meet. Use directions to describe this location.
This location is in Canada, northeast of Maine.

8. What state appears west of about 71°W longitude?
New Hampshire

9. Which general direction would you travel from the city of Portland to the coordinate 45°N latitude, 68°W longitude?
northeast

10. What river extends in a north/south direction between 69° and 70°W longitude?
the Kennebec River

85

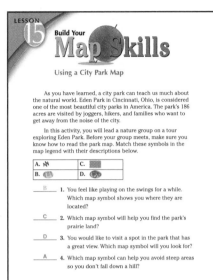

LESSON 15
Build Your Map Skills
Using a City Park Map

As you have learned, a city park can teach us much about the natural world. Eden Park in Cincinnati, Ohio, is considered one of the most beautiful city parks in America. The park's 186 acres are visited by joggers, hikers, and families who want to get away from the noise of the city.

In this activity, you will lead a nature group on a tour exploring Eden Park. Before your group meets, make sure you know how to read the park map. Match these symbols in the map legend with their descriptions below.

| A. | | C. | |
| B. | | D. | |

B 1. You feel like playing on the swings for a while. Which map symbol shows you where they are located?

C 2. Which map symbol will help you find the park's prairie land?

D 3. You would like to visit a spot in the park that has a great view. Which map symbol will you look for?

A 4. Which map symbol can help you avoid steep areas so you don't fall down a hill?

88

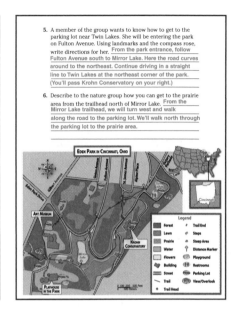

5. A member of the group wants to know how to get to the parking lot near Twin Lakes. She will be entering the park on Fulton Avenue. Using landmarks and the compass rose, write directions for her. From the park entrance, follow Fulton Avenue south to Mirror Lake. Here the road curves around to the northeast. Continue driving in a straight line to Twin Lakes at the northeast corner of the park. (You'll pass Krohn Conservatory on your right.)

6. Describe to the nature group how you can get to the prairie area from the trailhead north of Mirror Lake. From the Mirror Lake trailhead, we will turn west and walk along the road to the parking lot. We'll walk north through the parking lot to the prairie area.

89

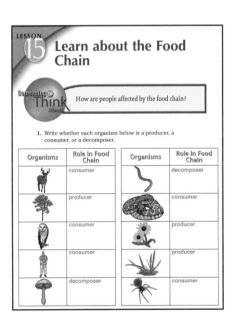

LESSON 15
Learn about the Food Chain

Something to Think About
How are people affected by the food chain?

1. Write whether each organism below is a producer, a consumer, or a decomposer.

Organisms	Role in Food Chain	Organisms	Role in Food Chain
	consumer		decomposer
	producer		consumer
	consumer		producer
	consumer		producer
	decomposer		consumer

90

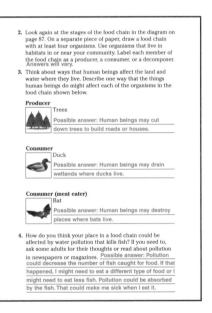

2. Look again at the stages of the food chain in the diagram on page 87. On a separate piece of paper, draw a food chain with at least four organisms. Use organisms that live in habitats in or near your community. Label each member of the food chain as a producer, a consumer, or a decomposer. Answers will vary.

3. Think about ways that human beings affect the land and water where they live. Describe one way that the things human beings do might affect each of the organisms in the food chain shown below.

Producer
Trees
Possible answer: Human beings may cut down trees to build roads or houses.

Consumer
Duck
Possible answer: Human beings may drain wetlands where ducks live.

Consumer (meat eater)
Bat
Possible answer: Human beings may destroy places where bats live.

4. How do you think your place in a food chain could be affected by water pollution that kills fish? If you need to, ask some adults for their thoughts or read about pollution in newspapers or magazines. Possible answer: Pollution could decrease the number of fish caught for food. If that happened, I might need to eat a different type of food or I might need to eat less fish. Pollution could be absorbed by the fish. That could make me sick when I eat it.

91

Notes